CLASSIC KOREAN TALES
with commentaries

CLASSIC KOREAN TALES

with commentaries

Choe Key-sook

Carlsbad, CA and Seoul

Classic Korean Tales, with commentaries

Copyright © 2018 by Choe Key-sook

Translated by Lee Sun-hee & Allison Blodgett
Poetry translations edited by Ko Yu-jin
Illustrated by Lee Hyun-a

Edited by Ha Soon-young, Hahm Min-ji, Chae Hyeon-a
Designed by You Ye-ji

All rights reserved.
No part of this book may be used in any form,
without prior written permission from the copyright holders.

First published in 2018
Second printing, 2021
by Hollym International Corp., Carlsbad, CA, USA
Phone 760 814 9880
http://www.hollym.com   **e-Mail** contact@hollym.com

Published simultaneously in Korea
by Hollym Corp., Publishers, Seoul, Korea
Phone +82 2 734 5087   **Fax** +82 2 730 5149
http://www.hollym.co.kr   **e-Mail** hollym@hollym.co.kr

ISBN : 978-1-56591-489-6
Library of Congress Control Number: 2017963342

Printed in Korea

A Way of Communicating with Time: The World of Korean Classical Imagination

When did you start reading and why? A book can provide you with a sense of direction. It can contain your dreams and hopes, and provide you with a sense of yourself. However, someone else has written the books that you have selected. How is it possible that reading a book becomes an opportunity to meet yourself and becomes a way to gain insight into how to live your life? The book you are reading or about to read is not one you have written, but you are the one who reads and understands the story, becomes moved, gains wisdom, or falls into deep contemplation. What you come to understand and feel by reading a book is similar to writing a new volume of that book. If you become curious about the behavior of main characters and share their sorrows and pleasures while reading a book, you walk on the same path as the writer and swim in the same sea of feelings. The sense of empathy you develop while reading is similar to the feeling you get while listening to music you like; you nod or shake your shoulders and move your feet to the rhythm and feel that you have become one with the player.

The story world that you newly encounter through reading sometimes plays an important role in your life. For example, a book's world has a great effect on you when you gain courage or necessary wisdom from that book. In addition, when you feel that the main character is similar to you or is someone you are afraid of or dislike, it means that you are finding yourself in the book, and furthermore, that you are coming to understand humans as they are. In this respect, reading is not only a pleasant journey in which you find out who you are, but it can also be a chapter in which you learn about things in life that are difficult, but that you need to know. While trying to assimilate a story world or understand it, you decide your attitude toward life and what kind of person you want to be. In that sense, reading is not only a discovery of yourself, but also a precious experience that forms your future.

The olden days of past captured in the classics have disappeared in the flow of time, but in these stories, the dreams and hopes, worries and sadness, and pleasure and joy of the people from that time remain. A lonely boy becomes a hero who establishes a nation; a daughter who is abandoned becomes a goddess who manages death; a wife and husband, both ordinary people, become a queen and king in a foreign country or gods of a country. These stories show you that if people take advantage of their merits and use their power in support of others, they can accomplish wonderful things and gain happiness even when they possess nothing special.

The reason that these stories survive for such a long time without being forgotten and move the people who read them is that people consider the thoughts and feelings in these stories to be precious. What brings "classics" alive is the readers' empathy.

The world of classics, which appears interesting and mysterious, also contains the dreams and hopes of contemporary people. Even though the past has disappeared, you are encountering the dreams and hopes of people from olden times as you read the classics and fall into the world of these stories. Reading the classics is similar to the experience of communicating across time. If the world that came from people's imagination in the old days is not different from your world of imagination, you will discover that some aspects of people and life are constant over time. If you find that people these days behave differently than people in the old days, you will come to realize that some aspects of humanity change over the flow of time and you will experience that change. You will discover the elements that should not change over time and also what should not be missed in the flow of historical change. If this book can show you how to time travel and the way the world flows becomes clearer and appears more virtuous to you, I believe this will be a great intellectual reward for everyone, including those who wrote these stories, those who crafted them into a book, and those who read them.

Lastly, I would like to deliver my deepest gratitude to the editor Ha Soon-young, at Hollym Publisher; and the Illustrator Lee Hyun-a; co-translators, Lee Sun-hee and Allison Blodgett; and Ko Yu-jin, who worked hard to transfer thoughts in-depth and to provide an enriched sensibility of *Classic Korean Tales* to English readers. I hope that readers of this book may fully appreciate thinking about universality, historicity, and locality in classic Korean literature.

Choe Key-sook

Contents

Preface · 5

Narratives about Origins and the World of Myths

The Myth of King Dongmyeong · 16
Commentaries
A Heroic Founder of a Nation's Leadership and Reign:
the Myth of King Dongmyeong · 34

The Myth of Princess Bari · 46
Commentaries
Princess Bari, Deserted by People —
Nonetheless Became a Goddess · 82

Yeonohrang and Seonyeo · 98
Commentaries
The People are Heaven · 102

Stories of Love and Marriage

Seodong and Princess Seonhwa · 112
Commentaries
Streets, Music, and the Cultural Politics of Children's Song · 116

The Idiot Ondal and Princess Pyeonggang · 124
Commentaries
Cultural Politics of Sensibility Crossing Over Differences and Borders · 130

Domi and His Wife · 138
Commentaries
The Domi's Love and Trust · 142

Beautiful Person, Beautiful Mind

Madam Suro · 152
Commentaries
Madam Suro, the Goddess of Beauty and Treasure of Silla · 156

The Filial Daughter Jieun · 162
Commentaries
Ethics of Filial Piety and Cultural Politics · 166

The World of Fantasy

Josin's Dream · **176**
    Commentaries
    Josin's Dream, Introspective Reflection of Desire · 182

Kim Hyeon Gam Ho:
The Love between Kim Hyeon and a Lady Tiger · **188**
    Commentaries
    Love of a Lady Tiger that is more Humanistic than that of Humans · 194

Yi Saeng Gyu Jang Jeon:
The Story of Yi Saeng Peering Over the Wall · **202**
    Commentaries
    A House of a Ghost, Ontology of Extinction · 226

Epilogue · 238

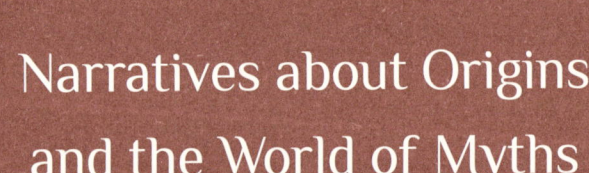

Narratives about Origins and the World of Myths

- The Myth of King Dongmyeong
- The Myth of Princess Bari
- Yeonohrang and Seonyeo

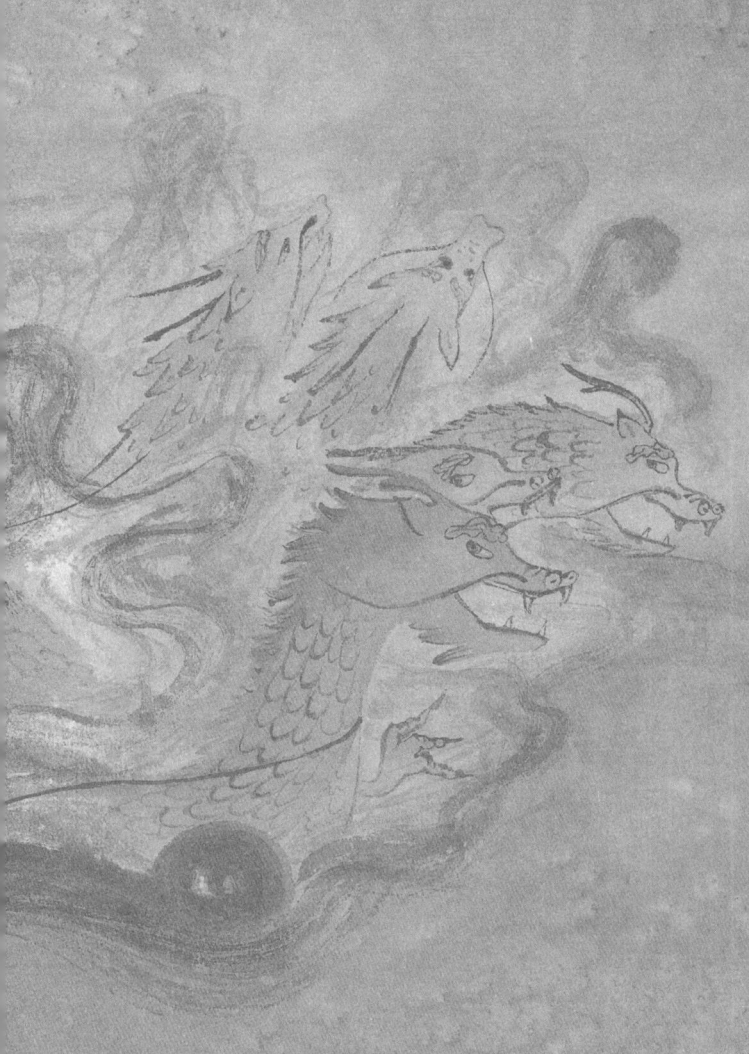

"I am a grandson of God and also of Habaek. As I have come here to avoid misfortune, Heaven and Earth, please have sympathy and quickly send me a boat and a bridge."

Upon saying that, Jumong struck the water with his bow. Fish and soft shelled turtles then emerged from the water forming a bridge for him.

Excerpted from ⟨The Myth of King Dongmyeong⟩

What was the first story to appear in the world? When was it composed? Why did people make up stories and love to talk about them? If you have ever had an interest in these issues, it means that you have already thought about the origins of literature. Ultimately, all these questions are related to a question about "myths," which were the first stories ever made.

Mythology is the system of thought that provides an explanation of the origin of the world's creatures and their principles of existence in terms of stories. Myths are the oldest among the various forms of stories. Even before humans had writing systems, myths existed through an oral tradition; it is the oldest form of literature. The reason we call the Korean stories *sinhwa* ("myth") is that these stories are commonly about the birth of *sin* ("gods"). In summary, myths are generally narratives about origins; they express or convey knowledge of origins or births in terms of stories. "Narratives" refers to "stories."

The stories in this book, including ⟨The Myth of King Dongmyeong⟩, ⟨The Myth of Princess Bari⟩, and ⟨Yeonohrang and Seonyeo⟩, talk about the origin of a great variety of things in the world, including a great nation, a hero, a goddess of the dead, the sun and the moon, etc. They also talk about the process by which laws of the universe are formed.

⟨The Myth of King Dongmyeong⟩ is a story about the birth of a nation called Goguryeo and a story about its founder Jumong. ⟨The Myth of Princess Bari⟩ is a story that answers a question about origin: "What happens when people die and where do we go?" Through myths, people tried to resolve their curiosity about death and to overcome their fear of it. ⟨Yeonohrang and Seonyeo⟩ is a myth about the sun and the moon, which means it is a myth about the formation of the universe.

If while reading these stories, you can empathize with the meaning and spirit of these myths and appreciate the deep beauty they contain, it will be possible to define myths as a form of contemporary literature and culture, still alive and ongoing.

The Myth of King Dongmyeong

A long, long time ago, there was a minister named Aranbul in Buk-Buyeo (North Buyeo). One day, Aranbul had a strange dream. In his dream, God appeared to him and said, "One of my descendants will come to the land of Buyeo and build a country. Therefore, you must leave this land."

The dream was so vivid and real that Aranbul could not shake his memory of it. Since he could not go against God's will, he searched for a place to move after leaving Buyeo.

Near the East Coast, there was a land called Gaseopwon. It was appealing with fertile soil for farming crops and a pleasant climate desirable for living. Aranbul went to Haeburu, the king of Buk-Buyeo, and said, "I met with God in my dream last night, and he told me to leave this land because his descendant will build a country in the land of Buyeo. I have scouted the area and found a place with fertile soil named Gaseopwon near the East Coast. It will be worthwhile to make it the capital city."

King Haeburu also could not refuse an order from the Lord, so he

The Myth of King Dongmyeong

moved the capital city to Gaseopwon and changed the name of the country to Dong-Buyeo (East Buyeo) from Buk-Buyeo (North Buyeo).

King Haeburu was old and he didn't have a son. He prayed with great sincerity to all the gods of the mountains and rivers for one. One day while traveling by horseback, Haeburu reached a pond called Gonyeon. As his horse gazed upon a large rock near the pond, the horse started to shed tears. Haeburu thought that this was strange and asked his servant to roll the rock over. There a small child resembling a golden frog appeared. The king said, "This child is the son who Heaven has sent to me."

The king took the child and named him Geumwa meaning "golden frog." Haeburu made Geumwa the crown prince. When the king died, Geumwa ascended to the crown and became the king. After Haeburu moved the capital of Buk-Buyeo and changed the name of the country to Dong-Buyeo, God asked his crown prince, Haemosu, to go and stay in the old capital of Buk-Buyeo.

Haemosu came down from the sky in a splendid carriage pulled by five dragons. Behind the carriage, there were hundreds of followers riding on white swans. Colorful clouds floated around them and the air pulsated magnificently with beautiful music. Haemosu and his followers landed on

Mt. Ungsim and spent about ten days or so before finally descending to earth. Haemosu wore a crown decorated with crow feathers on his head, holding a shining sword, Yonggwanggeom, at his waist. He ruled over the world in the morning and returned to the heavens in the evening.

At that time, Habaek, the god of water who rules over rivers, lived near the Aprok River. He had three beautiful daughters. The first was Yuhwa; the second, Hwonhwa; and the last, Wihwa. All of them were beautiful with delicate figures. The precious jewelry decorating their bodies rustled whenever they moved, with a pure and clear sound that was pleasant to listen to. They loved to come out of the Aprok River and play near a pond on Mt. Ungsim.

One day, Haemosu, who was staying at the foot of Mt. Ungsim, happened to see Habaek's three daughters near the pond. With great admiration for the daughters' beauty, Haemosu said, "If I take one of them as my wife, I will be able to have an heir."

The vassals accompanying him added, "That is a brilliant idea!"

Haemosu nodded his head without a word.

One day, Habaek's three daughters left their father's territory, the Aprok River, as usual and went out to the pond on Mt. Ungsim. They were spending time playing there, when they saw Haemosu approaching on a splendidly decorated horse. The three daughters felt embarrassed and didn't know what to do. They rushed into the water to avoid Haemosu. Upon seeing this, Haemosu's vassals said, "My Majesty, please build a palace quickly inside the water. You can simply shut the gate when those women enter the palace."

Immediately, Haemosu faced the water and used a horse whip to draw the outline of a palace. The image then turned into a bronze palace. Upon entering the palace, Haemosu sat at the palace table and gave the order for food and drink to be prepared. Habaek's daughters, who were in the water, became curious and walked into the palace. Having seen the splendid and beautiful party at the palace, they approached Haemosu without fear. Haemosu introduced himself to them as the son of God. They had great fun together sharing glasses and they became drunk. However, Haemosu was only waiting for the moment when those three women would become overly intoxicated.

As the three ladies became increasingly drunk, fitting the mood of such a fun party, Haemosu suddenly changed his gentle attitude and moved in closer to them. Frightened by Haemosu's movements, Habaek's daughters started to run away from him. However, the first daughter, Yuhwa, failed to escape and was caught. From that time on, Haemosu and Yuhwa lived together in the palace and fell in love with each other.

Yuhwa's father, Habaek, discovered what happened and became furious. He sent a messenger and warned Haemosu, "Who are you? What kind of person dares to hold my daughter hostage?"

Upon listening to this remark, Haemosu sent a reply to Habaek, "I am the son of God. Now, I would like to propose to your daughter."

Habaek then sent the messenger again, "If you were really the son of God and wanted to propose to my daughter, you should have sent your mediator to propose. Instead, you have rudely taken her captive."

Haemosu felt ashamed for having stayed with Yuhwa without alerting Habaek. Hence, he visited Habaek himself. However, Habaek knew that Haemosu had not brought Yuhwa with him, so he would not allow him into his palace. Returning to his own palace, Haemosu decided to set Yuhwa free, but she was already madly in love with him and was not happy to hear that she could return home. After being silent for some time, she told Haemosu that there was a way for them to go home together. "If we have a carriage driven by a dragon, we can return home together."

Haemosu ordered the preparation of a mysterious holy carriage driven by a dragon, and he visited Habaek's palace with Yuhwa. Finally, Habaek formally welcomed Haemosu and Yuhwa with honor. After they had all seated themselves, Habaek asked, "There are rules to follow for marriage. Why did you not follow the rules and insult my family?"

Haemosu kept silent. Then Habaek continued again, "I have heard that you became the king because you are the son of God. What kind of abilities do you have?"

Haemosu replied, "If you really want to know, please feel free to test me in your own way."

Habaek stepped into a pond in front of a garden and turned into a carp. He began to swim on the waves. Haemosu then changed into an otter and tried to catch the carp. Habaek changed into a deer and attempted to run away. Haemosu transformed into a wild dog and chased the deer. Habaek then changed into a pheasant, and Haemosu became a hawk and attacked the pheasant. After all of these, Habaek could admit that Haemosu was the son of God. He held a formal wedding ceremony for Haemosu and Yuhwa with full courtesies.

After the wedding, Habaek began to worry whether Haemosu would, by some chance, leave his first daughter, Yuhwa. So Habaek held a big party at which he let music play and invited Haemosu to drink a lot. Habaek's plan was to send a drunken Haemosu and Yuhwa to the heavens in a small palanquin on a cart led by a dragon.

A drunken Haemosu rode a palanquin on a cart, which was led by the dragon, as Habaek had planned, but at the moment the cart left the river, Habaek's territory, Haemosu woke up from the rumbling noise. Completely awakened, Haemosu quickly became aware of Habaek's plan. However, he had already planned to leave Yuhwa behind and to return to the heavens by himself, and he couldn't let Habaek's plan unfold. Grabbing a golden hair clip from Yuhwa's hair, Haemosu tore the leather cart and escaped flying up to the heavens alone.

Upon learning what had happened, Habaek became furious, but Haemosu had already left. Habaek scolded Yuhwa, who was left behind. "You did not follow a father's lessons to his daughters and have finally brought insult to our family's name."

Habaek told the servants at his side to pull Yuhwa's lips and to tie them at the ends. Yuhwa's lips were stretched up to three *cheok*[1] as the ends of them were tied. Also, he ordered Yuhwa to be expelled to the pond Wubalsu on the south side of Mt. Taebaek. She was allowed only two servants. Exiled to Wubalsu, Yuhwa was forced to lead a

---

1 *Cheok* is a unit measuring height. One *cheok* is approximately one foot.

torturous life.

Wubalsu was the pond of Dong-Buyeo (East Buyeo), which was governed by King Geumwa. A farmer named Gangryeokbuchu lived there. He worked at catching fish by laying a net and served them to the king. He began to be very suspicious as small numbers of fish would suddenly disappear from the net. Finally, he spoke to King Geumwa.

"These days, there is something stealing fish from the net. I am not sure what animal it is."

King Geumwa ordered the fisherman to pull the net out. As expected, the net was torn here and there. The king asked him to make an iron net for next time and to put it in the pond and then pull it back. In this net appeared a woman sitting on a rock. The woman could not speak because of her long lips. After cutting her lips three times, she could speak. King Geumwa knew that she was the wife of God's son, Haemosu, so he had her stay in a separate royal residence.

The sunlight always chased Yuhwa and cast its light on her. Even though Yuhwa tried to avoid the light, it kept chasing her, shining light on her bosom. As a result, she became pregnant.

It was April of *gyehaenyeon*[2] in the lunar calendar, which is the 4th year of *Sinjak*.[3] An egg the size of five *dwe*[4] came from Yuhwa's armpit on her left-side. King Geumwa heard the news and thought

---

2   *Gyehaenyeon* is the 60th year of the sexagenary cycle, the year of the black pig.
3   *Sinjak* refers to the years of the 10th Emperor Seonje's reign in the Han dynasty from 61 BC to 58 BC.
4   *Dwe* is a unit measuring amount. One *dwe* is approximately 1.8 liters.

that it was strange. "It is not auspicious that a human has laid an egg like a bird."

The king asked people to move the egg to the horse barn. However, the horses neither ate it nor stepped on it. Next, he gave the order to throw it away deep inside the mountains, but all the animals protected the egg. Sunlight shone on the egg all the time even on cloudy days. The egg was unbreakable no matter how hard people tried. The king couldn't help but return the egg to its mother. Yuhwa wrapped the egg with a cloth and put it in a warm place.

Finally, the egg hatched and out came a child. His cry was very loud and his physique and appearance were outstanding and mysterious. Even before the end of his first month, he started to speak and his speech was flawless.

One day, the child told his mother, "Mother, flies are licking my eyes, and I cannot fall asleep. Please make arrows for me."

Mother made arrows from bamboo branches and gave them to the child. With those arrows, he shot at some flies on a cart and hit every one of them. In those days, a great archer was called "Jumong" in Buyeo. Since Yuhwa's child was good at archery, he was called "Jumong." As Jumong grew up, he had various sorts of talents.

King Geumwa had seven sons. They always played with Jumong and went hunting together, but they couldn't compete with Jumong's talents. One day, the princes went out hunting with Jumong. While the princes caught a deer with about forty servants, Jumong captured several by himself with arrows. The princes became jealous and tied Jumong to a tree. They snatched his deer and returned home.

Jumong then returned home with the uprooted tree. This made the princes even more jealous of Jumong and they hated him. The first prince, Daeso, said to King Geumwa, "Jumong is a strong man, and he is mysterious and brave. He has ambition in his eyes, and he is not a common man. If you do not get rid of him right away, you will definitely regret it later."

King Geumwa ordered Jumong to take care of the horses in order to test him. Jumong grew spitefulness at being made to raise horses, and he went to talk to his mother. "I am a grandchild of God. It is better for me to die than to live taking care of horses for other people. I would like to build a country in the southern land, but because you are here, I cannot do anything that I want to do."

His mother, Yuhwa, answered, "Is that why you have been worried day and night? I have heard that a strong horse is necessary for a strong man to travel a long way. I am able to pick out that horse."

Yuhwa explained to Jumong how to select a strong horse. Jumong then went to the barn and randomly beat horses here and there with a long whip. The frightened horses started to run away. Among them was a red horse that jumped over a fence more than two *gil*[5] high. Jumong noticed that this horse was the best one, and he impaled the root of the horse's tongue with a needle. Because of the pain in its tongue, the horse could not drink water or eat grass, and it became weaker and weaker every day.

It was the day that King Geumwa came to check on the horse

---

5   *Gil* is a unit measuring length. One *gil* corresponds to 10 or 8 *ja* (One *ja* is a Korean foot and is equal to 30.3cm).

barn. He looked around and was very pleased to see all the stout horses, except one. The king told Jumong to take that skinny horse. Jumong took the horse home, removed the needle from its tongue, and fed it well.

One day, Jumong's mother, Yuhwa, found out that the seven princes, including the first son, Daeso, and their servants were planning to kill Jumong. She called Jumong and advised him, "Some people in this country are trying to eliminate you. You have outstanding talent and wisdom, and you will survive wherever you go. Please leave here as soon as you can." However, Jumong could not leave his mother behind. As she realized that her son had a tender heart, mother told him, "Do not worry about me."

Yuhwa gave Jumong seeds of five grains. Jumong was to sow the seeds and eat them wherever he settled down. Jumong said goodbye to his mother and started the journey in haste with three friends: Oi, Mari, and Hyeopbo. When they reached the bank of the Eomsu River, they tried to cross the river, but didn't have a boat. Because Daeso and his party were chasing them, Jumong was anxious and in a hurry. Standing near the riverside, Jumong lamented with a sigh, pointing to the heavens with a horsewhip, "I am a grandson of God and also of Habaek. As I have come here to avoid misfortune, Heaven and Earth, please have sympathy and quickly send me a boat and a bridge."

Upon saying that, Jumong struck the water with his bow. Fish and soft shelled turtles then emerged from the water forming a bridge for him. Using that bridge, Jumong was able to cross the river. Later, the soldiers chasing Jumong arrived. When they tried to cross the bridge of fish and soft shelled turtles, it abruptly collapsed. Those who had already been on the bridge fell into the river and drowned.

After safely crossing the river, Jumong took a short rest under a big tree. It then occurred to him that he had left home without the seeds of five grains that his mother had wrapped for him. He had forgotten to take them while saying a sad goodbye to his mother. As Jumong pitied his situation, a pair of doves flew to him. Jumong said, "They are the seeds of five grains that my mother has sent." Jumong hit the doves with arrows. Each shot made an exact hit. The mouths of the doves were filled with seeds of five grains. Removing those seeds, he sprinkled water on the doves. They then came back to life and flew away.

Jumong reached Modungok and encountered three people. One of them wore clothes made of hemp cloth, another wore monk's clothes, and the last one wore clothes made of reeds. All of them looked very shabby. Jumong asked them, "Where are you from? What are your last names and first names?"

The man in hemp cloth said,

"My name is Jaesa."

The man in a monk's uniform said,

"My name is Mugol."

Then the man in clothing made of reeds said,

"My name is Mukgeo."

However, they did not reveal their last names. Jumong assigned them their last names, for Jaesa, Geuk; for Mogol, Jungsil; and for

Mukgeo, Sosil. Jumong told his followers, "I received an order from Heaven, and now I intend to launch the foundation of a country. Since I have met these wise men at the right time, this clearly means God helps me."

After identifying their abilities, Jumong assigned them jobs and reached Jolboncheon with them. (According to the Chinese history book *Wiseo*, he arrived at Heulseunggolseong.) The soil was rich and the scenery was beautiful, while the mountains and rivers were wild providing protection. Thus, Jumong decided to make Jolboncheon the capital city and to settle down there. Without enough time to build a palace, he lived in a hut near the bank of the Biryu River. He entitled the country "Goguryeo" and ascended the throne himself. He also took "Go" as his last name. Jumong was twenty-two years old at this time. (With respect to this period, *Wiseo* says, "Jumong arrived at Jolbon-Buyeo. The king of Jolbon-Buyeo did not have a son, and he gave his daughter to Jumong because he found Jumong extraordinary. After the king died, Jumong succeeded to the throne.") That year was the 2nd year of *Geonso*[6] and also the 21st year of the first king in Silla, King Hyeokgeose.

There were many followers who had heard about Goguryeo and Jumong and who gathered from all over the place. As the land was close to the Malgal[7] villages, people in Goguryeo were worried about attack and robbery from Malgal. Because of this concern, Goguryeo attacked the Malgal first. The Malgal then surrendered in fear and

---

6   *Geonso* refers to the years of the 11th Emperor Hyowonje's reign in the Han dynasty.
7   Magal is a Tungusic people who lived in northeast Asia.

dared not invade them.

One day, the king of Goguryeo saw vegetable leaves floating down the river, and he noticed that there were people living in the district upriver. The king visited that district on the way to hunting. The land was the country Biryu and the king was Songyang. At the same time, King Songyang, who was also on his way to hunting, saw Jumong and noticed that he was an extraordinary figure. Songyang arranged a meeting with Jumong and said, "Because our country is located at the edge of the seashore, I did not have occasion to meet you before today. However, it is very fortunate that I can finally meet with you. Who are you? And where are you from?"

The king of Goguryeo replied, "I am a grandson of God and the king of Goguryeo located in the west. I dare to ask you, but whose descendant are you?"

King Songyang then answered, "I am a descendant of a Taoist hermit. From generation to generation, the kings have come from our family. This place has such a small land for people to live in, but has two kings. However, we cannot divide the country, and I wonder what we should do. Since it is not so long ago that you built your country, what about becoming a tributary of our country?"

The king of Goguryeo then said, "I am a grandson of God. You are not even a descendant of God, yet you occupy the position of king. How is this possible? If you do not become a subordinate country of Goguryeo, God must punish you."

Upon hearing Jumong argue that he was a grandson of God, Songyang became suspicious. In order to test Jumong's capability, Songyang proposed, "I would like to compete in archery skills with you."

Songyang decided to draw a deer on a target and to shoot a bow at it from one hundred steps away. He concentrated and bent the bow to the full, but the arrow didn't even hit the belly of the deer, and Songyang was exhausted. Then it was Jumong's turn. He asked to hang a jade ring at the center of the target. He shot a bow from one hundred steps away. The arrow hit the jade dead center and broke into pieces. Songyang was shocked at what he saw.

After winning, Jumong returned to Goguryeo. Songyang, however, never yielded to Goguryeo and reigned over the country as the king of Biryu. It was a troublesome issue for Goguryeo to solve. The king of Goguryeo, Jumong, consulted with his vassals and said, "Even though Goguryeo has been newly formed, the rules of decorum for the country have not been established. Therefore, I could neither greet an envoy of the king of Biryu nor see him off with appropriate customs as king when he visited us. It is natural to greet envoys of neighboring countries by playing courteous music. However, Goguryeo does not have these established customs. Thus, the party from Biryu despises our country and me and considers us inferior because we do not have appropriate etiquette. Isn't this a serious problem?"

Then Bubunno serving King Jumong said, "Yes, it is. There is music for formal decorum in Biryu as well as proper musical instruments. Therefore, they seem to look down on our country for not having established manners. I will go to Biryu in person and bring back such an instrument."

Jumong asked, "How are you going to bring back such a precious thing, which is hidden deep in their country?"

"That instrument is given by God, so why would it be impossible for me to bring it to you? Whoever thought that your Majesty would build a country when you suffered bitter insults from Geumwa's seven sons and their groups in Buyeo? In spite of all the hardships, your Majesty overcame the difficulties and formed a nation. It is Heaven's order that your name be wielded all over the world after being rescued from various dangers. Therefore, what in the world can you not accomplish?"

Bubunno took some people to Biryu and brought the instrument back. Assuming that Goguryeo had taken the instrument, Biryu sent an envoy to Goguryeo and demanded its return. Because Jumong was worried that the envoy would expect the return of the instrument after seeing it, he painted the instrument dark and made it look old. The envoy couldn't help but return home without saying anything.

The king of Biryu did not give up the idea of having Goguryeo as a vassal state. Furthermore, taking advantage of the fact that Goguryeo had just been formed, the king proposed that a country with a longer history become the ruling country of a newly-built country. In turn, the king of Goguryeo ordered a palace to be built using rotten wood as pillars. In accordance with his order, the palace was built using rotten wood and looked as if it were more than a thousand years old. When visiting Goguryeo, Songyang couldn't argue that Biryu had a longer history and he had to go back. Henceforth, quarrels between Goguryeo and Biryu were never-ending.

One day, Jumong went hunting in the west and earned himself a white deer. He hung the deer upside down in a place called Haewon and gave the following order, "I will not set you free until God floods the capital of Biryu with rainfall. If you want to escape from this situation, appeal to God." Then the white deer cried sadly. The cry seemed to reach the heavens, and all of sudden, it began to pour in Biryu. The monsoon rains did not stop for seven days. The capital, which was governed by Songyang, became submerged under water. Songyang crossed the water using straw ropes made from weeds, and the people of Biryu hung onto the ropes. When Jumong appeared and struck the water with a whip, the surging water suddenly disappeared completely.

When it became summer, June of the lunar calendar, Songyang came to the king of Goguryeo and surrendered. Biryu became subjugated to Goguryeo.

July of the lunar calendar in the same year, dark clouds covered a mountain in a place called Gollyeong. As a result, people could not see the mountain. From inside, came a noise that thousands of people were building something. The king of Goguryeo, Jumong, said, "God is building a castle for me."

Seven days later, the clouds and fog naturally faded away. In the place where the mountain had been, castle walls and palaces had been built. The king bowed to the heavens, and he lived there governing the country.

Years later, it became the 19th year (19 BC) of Jumong's reign over the country. In April of the lunar calendar, Jumong made Prince Yuri the crown prince. September of the same year, the king passed away. He was forty years old. In Yeongsan, his funeral ceremony was splendidly conducted and he was named King Dongmyeong.

Origins   Lee Gyu-bo, ⟨*Dongmyeongwang*⟩, *Donggugisanggukjip*
Kim Bu-sik, 'Progenitor King Dongmyeongseong,' *vol.13*, ⟨*Goguryeobongi*⟩, *Samguksagi*
Ilyeon, 'Dong-buyeo,' 'Goguryeo,' ⟨*Kee*⟩, *Samgukyusa*

This story is written based on Lee's record of ⟨*King Dongmyeong*⟩ in *Donggukisanggukjip*, Kim's record of 'Dongmyeogseongwang' in ⟨*Goguryeobongi*⟩ of *Samguksagi*, and Ilyeon's record of Goguryeo Jumong's birth myth in ⟨*Kee*⟩ of *Samgukyusa*.

Commentaries

A Heroic Founder of a Nation's Leadership and Reign: the Myth of King Dongmyeong

The Origin Myth of a Nation: Political Legitimacy and the Support for a Hero

The Great King Dongmyeong is the founder of Goguryeo; his name is Jumong. His father is Haemosu, a son of God, and his mother is Yuhwa, a daughter of Habaek, a god of water. The process through which Jumong established Goguryeo was politically turbulent and mythologically interesting. Political conflicts and problems to be solved trigger confusion in society. However, they also present a golden opportunity for a hero to show his ability and gain recognition. Because myths allow for events more difficult than in reality or more unbelievable, the events unfold even more excitingly and dramatically. Myths present implications of political contexts, cultural metaphors, and literary imagination through various symbolic devices. In an origin myth, symbolic devices lead to political agreements to justify establishing a nation and to secure the outstanding capability of a hero who built a nation. Furthermore, the myth is recorded in history books so as to confirm the legitimacy of the process and to ensure it is passed down over time. The myth of King Dongmyeong is also called the myth of Jumong in accordance with the name of the hero, Jumong. This story has been recorded in many historical works of literature such as *Donggugisanggukjip*,[1] *Samguksagi*,[2] *Samgukyusa*,[3] etc.[4] Among them, Dong-Buyeo and Goguryeo in section *Kee* of *Samgukyusa* show fantastic and mythological characteristics. For this reason and because the story is very interesting, it has been produced as a modern television drama.

A poster of the drama *Jumong* (MBC 2006-2007). The drama portrays Jumong's life from the demolition of Gojoseon till the establishment of Goguryeo. It was very popular with a more than 50% viewer rate in Korea at that time.

---

1 *Donggugisanggukjip* is the collected work of Lee Gyu-bo, published in 1241, the 28th year of King Gojong in Goryeo. The book includes history as well as poems. The Myth of King Dongmyeong in the section *Dongmyeong-pyeon* in the book can be referred to as a hero narrative.

2 *Samguksagi* is a history book compiled by Kim Bu-sik, according to the king's order in 1145, the 23rd year of King Injong in Goguryeo. *Goguryeobongi* in *Samguksagi* records accurate historical facts of the story.

3 *Samgukyusa* is a history book written by a Buddhist monk Ilyeon in 1281, the 7th year of King Chungryeol in Goryeo. The stories of Dong-Buyeo and Goguryeo in section *Kee* of the book have strong fantastic and mythological characteristics.

4 The story in this volume is composed by combining and rewriting all three records, *King Dongmyeong* in *Donggugisanggukjip*, *Goguryeobongi* in *Samguksagi*, and *Kee* in *Samgukyusa*.

The Foundation of Goguryeo Provided by God

The hero in establishing Goguryeo is Jumong. The starting point of the origin myth of a nation goes back to Jumong's father and mother. It was the time recorded as "a long time ago," and a minister named Aranbul in Buk-Buyeo (North Buyeo) had a dream in which God appeared and told him to leave the land because his descendant would build a nation there. Aranbul shared the dream with King Haeburu of Buk-Buyeo. Haeburu, who thought that God's order could not be disobeyed moved his capital Gaseopwon. He also changed the name of the country to Dong-Buyeo (East-Buyeo).

From a modern perspective, it is strange that a king of a nation believed his vassal's recounting of his dream and decided to move the capital and change the name of his nation as a result. However, when we interpret it as literary symbolism and explore the metaphor of political contexts behind it, it is quite comprehensible. It is a sort of foreshadowing garnering justification for establishing Goguryeo in the land. It is a mythological device delivering the message that Goguryeo was reasonably and peacefully built by following God's will and that its neighboring country voluntarily collaborated and agreed with building the nation.

Haeburu, who moved his capital, had no son. He performed a sincere ritual, praying to all the gods in the mountains and rivers[5] for

---

[5] In Korea, there was a custom of praying to gods of mountains and rivers in order to conceive a child. We can confirm that the origin of that practice goes back to the time period before Goguryeo. This practice reflects the human perspective of viewing the birth of a person as harmony and adaptation with nature and gods.

a son. One day, while on the way somewhere on horseback, he found a child in a pond called Gonyeon and brought him to the palace. It was the horse who found the child first and not Haeburu. The horse suddenly stopped and shed tears in front of a rock. As the rock was rolled back, there appeared a child looking like a golden frog. Haeburu named him Geumwa[6] and made him the crown prince. This part can be politically interpreted as Haeburu giving his throne not to a biological son but to a stepson. In the myth, Geumwa took care of Jumong's mother, Yuhwa, while raising her son, Jumong.

A Story before Jumong's Birth: Haemosu, Habaek, and Yuhwa

What did the God who made Haeburu leave the land of Buk-Buyeo do next? The God sent his crown prince Haemosu to the old capital of Buk-Buyeo. Haemosu came down from the sky in a splendid carriage pulled by five dragons. Behind the carriage, there were hundreds of followers riding on white swans. This scene is portrayed beautifully and in grandiose fashion. Haemosu displayed his dignified appearance and appeared perfectly suitable for taking up the capital of Buk-Buyeo.

He met Habaek's daughter, Yuhwa. This process is somewhat problematic from the modern perspective. It is because he was attracted to Habaek's daughters that he held them. In addition, from

---

6   Geumwa (金蛙) in Chinese characters literally means a golden frog.

the very beginning, he had no intention of taking one of the women, with whom he had a secret relationship as his wife, to the heavens.

Haemosu had the outstanding capability of building a palace in the water by brandishing a horse whip. The three daughters had a great time there without realizing Haemosu's scheme, and they became drunk. As Haemosu approached these women, they were startled and began to run away. Then, the first daughter Yuhwa, who could not escape, was seized by Haemosu. While living with him, she fell in love with him. From that time on, Yuhwa's father, Habaek, felt enraged because Haemosu stayed with Yuhwa without his permission.

After introducing himself to Habaek as God's son, Haemosu asked to marry Yuhwa. At first, Habaek did not meet with Haemosu, who had visited him in person. Habaek was not impressed by the fact that Haemosu was the son of God and asked him for proper courtesy, procedures, and customs. While Haemosu was controlling the power of the heavens, Habaek was controlling the power of rivers, and it was Yuhwa who mediated the two. She knew the laws of rivers belonging to her father and also the laws of the heavens through her marriage with Haemosu. Yuhwa informed Haemosu how to open Habaek's mind. She told him to make a formal visit to Habaek in a palanquin on a cart that was led by a dragon. Habaek wanted to see Haemosu not as a man but as the heir of heavenly God. In other words, he wanted a diplomatic relation, not a personal relation, which Haemosu accepted.

Habaek asked Haemosu, who wanted to marry his daughter, to

prove his ability. His request was for Haemosu to demonstrate his substantial capabilities, even though he admitted Haemosu as the son of God. Habaek ultimately acknowledged Haemosu's talent and allowed the marriage. Yet Habaek could not trust Haemosu. He felt that Haemosu might go up to the heavens someday leaving his daughter alone. (It turned out later that his worry was not groundless.) Habaek set up a plan: he hosted a party, intoxicated Haemosu, and sent him to the heavens with Yuhwa in a palanquin on a cart led by a dragon. However, as soon as he began to sober up, Haemosu saw through Habaek's plot. He then grabbed Yuhwa's hairpin, tore the leather cart, and flew up to the heavens.

Habaek scolded Yuhwa in fury because she had disgraced her family. He issued an order to stretch her lips and tie them, and to desert her in Wubalsu, a pond at the foot of Mt. Taebaek. Yuhwa was abandoned by her husband and also by her own father.

The Process of Jumong's Birth: Geumwa, Yuhwa, and Jumong

The place where Yuhwa was exiled belonged to the land of Dong-Buyeo (East Buyeo). A fisherman in the village experienced strange happenings; the fish that he had caught disappeared. In order to solve the problem, he visited King Geumwa. When the king ordered the net to be pulled out, Yuhwa appeared inside of it. The daughter of Habaek, god of rivers, survived at the bottom of the pond with fish stolen from the fisherman. Geumwa quickly noticed that she was Haemosu's queen, and he gave her a separate royal residence. Then a mysterious thing happened. The sunlight always chased her and cast its light on her back, and she became pregnant.

Time passed by and Yuhwa laid an egg from her left armpit. Saying that it was ominous that a human laid an egg, King Geumwa ordered it to be abandoned. Then various animals protected the egg. The sunlight always shone on top of it. The king couldn't help but return the egg to Yuhwa. The baby born from the egg was Jumong.

The scenes of Yuhwa's pregnancy and delivery have implications. The man who took care of the child was Geumwa, but the man who claimed to be his father was Haemosu. Haemosu imprinted his existence by appearing as the sunlight. Geumwa attempted to desert the child; Haemosu protected him till the end. This symbolizes that Haemosu claimed himself as Jumong's father biologically and socially.

How did Jumong Become a Hero for Building a Nation

Jumong had displayed his outstanding abilities since he was young. For instance, he was excellent in archery to the extent that he shot a fly that bothered him while napping. "Jumong" literally meant 'a great archer' in Goguryeo dialect at that time. His nickname became a real name.

King Geumwa had seven sons. They were all jealous of Jumong.

The Myth of King Dongmyeong

A Hunting Scene of Goguryeo Tomb Mural

Even though they all joined together and oppressed him, Jumong was strong and confident. Then, the first son Daeso incited his father. He advised him that there would be trouble in the future if the king did not eliminate Jumong. Jealousy framed the seed of slander.[7] King Geumwa asked Jumong to raise horses in order to test him, which was a chore. Jumong complained to Yuhwa that merely raising horses was too great an insult for his status, the grandson of God. He never forgot in his mind that he was the offspring of God in spite of the oppression from Daeso and his brothers. Then Jumong expressed his will to build a nation.

Yuhwa told Jumong how to acquire a swift horse. After Jumong

---

7   In the history of Korean classics, the motifs in which jealousy is the starting point of slander have been discussed as a constant theme.

raised a horse that had appeared gaunt because he had put a needle in its tongue, Geumwa gave the horse to him.[8] Yuhwa, who was abandoned by her husband and father and lived under Geumwa's protection, still had an outstanding ability and used it for the son. This horse played an important role by saving Jumong's life when Jumong's group was chased by Daeso's troops.

In the myth, Jumong demonstrated his ability and talent and maintained his self-esteem in spite of hardships and oppression. Without showing off his capability, he nurtured and improved it. In the end, he waited for the right timing and used his power for his ambition and dream. There was a moment when Jumong hit the water with a bow while escaping by riding on the horse. Just in time, fish and soft shelled turtles helped him by making a bridge for him.

Archery was Jumong's natural talent. Yet, water symbolizes his mother's country, i.e. his matrilineal power. In establishing a nation, Jumong's own power was crucial, but his mother Yuhwa's dynamic role cannot be excluded. Yuhwa sent seeds of five grains when Jumong left, which is very symbolic. She did not give him cooked rice, but seeds that he could plant and raise himself. This act is a mother's role in raising a hero.

Jumong had not brought the seeds his mother had given him. Then a pair of doves flew in. He hit these doves and found the seeds of five grains inside of them. Yuhwa wisely delivered the seeds to her

---

8 A story in which an excellent hero hides his abilities by only showing common behaviors appears in Korean lore. The structure of a story in which a hero looks like an idiot represents Korean ethics and sensibility in respecting hidden values of ordinary people.

son. If Jumong never noticed his mother's will and did not have the ability to hit the doves with an arrow, he could not have taken the seeds. He was able to become a hero because his capability and sense coordinated with Yuhwa's wisdom.

After taking the seeds, Jumong revived the doves. This symbolizes that he is not a blindly ambitious man and does not hesitate to kill for his purpose. Jumong, who resembled his mother, had the capability of caring and ethics to repay one's kindness. He possessed good judgment of human nature in recognizing talented people and keeping faithful relationships while appointing the talented to the right places. Skill in managing people is a necessary quality of political leaders.

When Jumong left Geumwa's land, he left with Oi, Mari, and Hyeopbo. They were Jumong's reliable friends and the founding contributors who helped in the establishment of Goguryeo. After leaving his hometown, Jumong met three other people in Modungok. They were shabbily dressed and had only first names, no last names. Jumong gave them last names and appointed them according to their ability. Those people did their parts through their lives as trustworthy vassals without betraying Jumong.

After Establishing Goguryeo, Jumong Became a Magnificent Leader

Jumong built a hut near the side of the Biryu River and entitled the country Goguryeo. He appointed himself as the king of Goguryeo. He also took the first character of the nation 'Go' as his last name. He took his last name not from his father or mother but from the country he established.

From a different perspective, Jumong was an insignificant and poor person. Above all, he was a child whose mother gave birth alone without a father. Even though King Geumwa raised him, Jumong was an outsider expelled because of jealousy from Geumwa's sons.[9] He was a loner for whom only fish, soft shelled turtles, and animals were on his side. Those who followed him were low class people wandering the world without family names. However, Jumong always felt proud that he was a grandson of God. He trained his skill in archery and used it as a resource in establishing a country.

With respect to seeking his mother's advice, he was an independent subject who maintained a proper distance to her and made his own judgements. He was also an ethical subject who treated people with respect and animals with generosity. He was an administrator who prepared for laws in the process of building a nation. When he built Goguryeo in the Biryu River,[10] its beginning was insignificant. However, he grew up to be a hero with outstanding ability, administrative skills, leadership, and diplomatic capability. The process of his fight, embracement, and collaboration with

---

9 When we consider Geumwa not as the stepfather, but as the biological father, jealousy against Jumong can be interpreted as exclusive enmity against step brothers.

10 It is assumed to be the river in the land of Goguryeo, the upper region of the Hunjiang River in Manchuria. There is a theory that Goguryeo's founder Jumong built a castle in the west side Holbon valley near this river.

King Songyang[11] symbolically demonstrates how he solidified the foundation of Goguryeo as a political, diplomatic, and military leader. Extraordinary transformation skills and the magical power to move nature are important mythological devices for mystifying Jumong's ability.

---

11 King Songyang is the king of Biryu, which is in nearby Goguryeo. Later, Biryu became annexed to Goguryeo.

The Myth of Princess Bari

This is a story that happened a long, long time ago in our land. These were the days when we could talk to the sun, the moon, and the stars in the sky, and when we could also go to the land of the dead.

At that time, a King Ogu lived in the land. He was not married, and he wanted to become a better ruler by having a queen, who would be the mother of the country. King Ogu called one of his court maids and asked her to visit a shaman worshipping a god, in order to obtain his fortune and schedule an auspicious date for a wedding.

The lady of the court followed the king's order and visited Cheonha Palace to meet the shaman who was worshipping the god. The shaman tossed grains of white rice on a table and remained silent with a very serious look on her face as if she were listening to the god's will. She then said, "The king is seventeen years old this year and the prospect queen is sixteen. If you hold the wedding this year, you will have a princess. But if you marry next year, you will have three princes. Please tell the king what I have said exactly as I have said it."

The servant reported to the king what she had heard from the shaman. King Ogu fell deep into thought for a moment and then opened his mouth to speak, "Even if her fortune telling is fairly amazing, how could she predict everything correctly? One day seems as if it is ten days, and one moment is three years to me, so I am in a rush. Please call all the officials and court ladies and prepare to welcome a new queen."

Because the king's order was firm, the officials and court ladies made haste in selecting a spouse for the king. It was right before Chilwol Chilseok, the 7th day of July in the lunar calendar, the day each year when Gyeonwu and Jiknyeo meet and then share their love. Thus, the officials decided upon Chilwol Chilseok, the day for uniting couples in love, as the wedding day, and they started to prepare for the wedding. Court maids and ladies spent extremely busy days decorating the queen's palace and finishing all the preparations for welcoming the queen.

Finally, Chilwol Chilseok, the wedding day, arrived. King Ogu, wearing splendid clothes and a dandy belt, and with gold and silver beads on his head and a graceful crown, greeted his bride, who was in gorgeous attire. The court maids and ladies in the upper garden bowed to them bending all the way over, and all the other officials, watching the wedding ceremony from the lower garden, sent their formal salute and congratulations on the wedding. King Ogu finished the ceremony to his full satisfaction and spent a sweet honeymoon with his beautiful queen, who was like a shy rose bud. The new title of "Madam Gildae" was given to the queen, which means "brightening the country forever."

After almost three years had passed since King Ogu and Madam Gildae had married, Madam Gildae experienced some changes in her body. She felt as if her bones were melting and her skeleton was twisted. She complained of pain everywhere and worried that something was wrong with her body. She also found it very hard to fall asleep at night. She refused to take any meals, complaining that soup smelled like soybean paste, and she felt quite uncomfortable because of the cold wind blowing through the window.

One day, Madam Gildae had a dream in which seven stars suddenly fell from the sky into her dress. It was so impressive and unlike a normal dream that she could not forget it. Because the dream was so strange, she shared it with King Ogu. The king summoned a court lady and asked her to find out what the dream meant.

In order to have Madam Gildae's dream interpreted, the court lady visited a shaman worshipping a god in Cheonha Palace. She brought five silver coins and five gold coins, as well as three *dwe* and three *hop*[1] of clean white rice in a clean and sacred cloth folded in three layers. The shaman unfolded a red scarf on a coral table, tossed grains of white rice, and shook a stick to receive the divination sign

---

[1] *Dwe* and *hop* are units for counting an amount of grain in Korea. One *hop* is a tenth of one *dwe* and corresponds to 180ml.

of the *Book of Changes*.[2] Then the shaman contemplated something before opening her mouth to speak, "The queen has become pregnant. However, because the wedding was held early, she will bear a princess."

The court lady reported to the king what she had heard. The king replied, "Even if her fortune telling is accurate, how could all her predictions be correct?"

A couple of months after Madam Gildae began showing symptoms of her pregnancy, the baby inside her collected blood and made the energy of life. It then settled down for three or four months in her womb and began to grow in good health. In the seventh month, King Ogu found a nanny to raise the baby and asked her to take care of Madam Gildae. He also made her prepare good herbs for the queen and to visit her three times a day, once every morning, day, and evening. After the eighth month and the ninth month passed, it finally became the tenth month. Madam Gildae finally gave birth to the baby. It was a beautiful, healthy princess.

Madam Gildae was so sad once she found out. The news was delivered to King Ogu and he also felt somewhat disappointed. In those days, the throne could only be inherited by a son, and so, King Ogu was expecting a son. However, he didn't express his feelings and said, "The queen has already given birth to a princess. Why not give birth to a prince later? Let's clean the queen's room, find a good wet nurse, and raise the baby by feeding her healthy milk."

---

2 The *Book of Changes* is one of the five ancient Chinese scriptures. The book presents 64 trigrams signifying philosophical, ethical, and political interpretations.

King Ogu named the baby Princess Byeolli (maening a star). Madam Gildae raised Byeolli with her unconditional love, but she felt disappointed in herself for having not delivered a son. Time went by and Byeolli turned three years old.

One day, Madam Gildae had a mysterious dream. In her dream, she went out to the backyard garden to see the flowers and broke the branch of a peach tree with her right hand. This dream was quite real and unforgettable, and again this time, she told King Ogu about the dream she had had. The king asked the court lady to learn what the dream indicated.

The lady visited Cheonha Palace to seek a fortune with five silver coins and five gold coins in a beautiful three-layered cloth. The shaman in Cheonha Palace unfolded a red scarf on a coral table, tossed grains of white rice, and read the fortune by picking up the trigrams of the *Book of Changes*. The shaman said, "With *Samsin*'s[3] help, the queen has become pregnant. However, she will have another princess."

The court lady delivered what she had heard to King Ogu. The king doubted it saying, "Even if her fortune telling is excellent, how could it be correct every time?"

The baby inside the queen collected blood for a couple of months, then settled down in the queen's womb for three or four months, and grew in good health. People in the court had busy days finding a court lady to take care of the queen and a wet nurse to feed the

---

3   *Samsin* is the goddess who decides who becomes pregnant.

newborn baby. The king sent someone to the pharmacy to find herbs for the queen and he also urged that someone should check the queen three times a day, morning, day, and evening. The eighth month and the ninth passed by, and finally, the baby was born in the tenth month. It was a princess. Madam Gildae was sad this time also.

Hearing the news, King Ogu hid his disappointment and said, "She already gave a birth to a princess; why wasn't she able to have a boy? Prepare a room for the princess in a nice place with a cozy bed. Select a good wet nurse and nourish the baby with her sweet milk."

King Ogu named his second daughter Princess Heuk (maening earth). Time passed by and Madam Gildae became pregnant again, while the princesses were growing up well. She felt her bones melting and her skeleton bending, while her bed was very uncomfortable. She couldn't eat because she smelled uncooked rice from the steamed rice and smelled plants from the marinated vegetables. She also sensed an odor of fermented soy beans in soup and the smell of mud from clams. She also shivered with cold from the wind blowing through the windows.

Madam Gildae had a dream this time also in which she saw the gold and jade beads of a crown. When she talked to the king about her dream, he said it was obvious that they would have a son this time, and he asked a court lady to go and consult a fortune teller quickly.

A court lady visited Cheonha Palace to see the fortune teller with five silver coins and five gold coins and a threefold cloth. The shaman unfolded a red cloth on a coral table, spread grains of white rice, and then selected the trigrams of the *Book of Changes*. "This time, the queen's baby comes from *Samsin*'s appointment and Buddha's guidance. However, it will be another princess."

The court lady delivered what she had heard; then the king said, "Even though her divination tends to be correct, how could it be right every time?"

The unborn baby grew in good health and was born in the tenth month. This time, it was also a princess. Madam Gildae could not hide her regret. The king heard the news and said without showing his pity, "She will have a son as she has already given birth to the princesses."

He ordered the princess entrusted to a nice nanny who would

raise her carefully. He named the baby Princess Ok (maening a jade).

Time flowed like a river. When the last baby turned five years old, Madam Gildae sensed a pregnancy again. She found her bed uncomfortable because her bones were melting and her skeleton bending. She smelled uncooked rice from steamed rice and plants from side dishes, and so she couldn't eat. Soup smelled like fermented soybean sauce and the clams like mud. She shivered because of the wind through the windows. The queen had dark freckles on her pretty face and was unable to look stylish with her fat waist. She was very weak and had a hard time with her loss of appetite, as she became susceptible to summer weather.

This time the queen also had an unforgettable dream. In her dream, a blue dragon and a gold dragon were cuddling together while winding over the girth of Daemyeong Chamber, the place in the palace where the king resided. She had a golden turtle sitting on her right knee and a silver turtle on the left. From her shoulders, the sun and the moon started to rise, while a blue crane and a white crane flew in and sat on her shoulders. After she told the king about her dream, he assured her that she would give birth to a son this time, and he asked to consult his fortune.

A court lady visited Cheonha Palace with five silver coins and five gold coins in a threefold cloth. The shaman in Cheonha Palace unfolded a red scarf on the coral table, spread grains of white rice, selected the trigrams of the *Book of Changes*, and then said, "This time the king will also have a princess."

When the court lady delivered what she had heard, the king said,

"Even though the divination tends to be correct, how could it be right every time? This time it is absolutely a boy."

King Ogu ordered preparations for welcoming a son because he was sure that this time there would be a son. He ordered a public notice announcing the news to be attached to the four main gates. He also rescinded the sentences of outcasts who had been exiled and he released prisoners from jail. He commanded that criminals would not be captured till the new baby was born. All these orders were done to celebrate the auspicious event.

The court ladies ground hundreds of fruits growing on the back hillside for the queen to drink. As the baby continued to grow well inside the queen's body, the court servants decorated a room for the new baby by cutting five hundred trees from the back hillside and trimming them carefully for ten days in the inner palace, where the queen resided. They were devoted to the queen and attended to her every day and carefully served herbs to her. They decided on a nanny and a wet nurse, who would nurture and breast-feed the baby, and they educated them while making them visit the queen and check on her health three times a day. The king also asked the court ladies not to leave the inner palace where the queen resided otherwise unattended. Finally, Madam Gildae gave birth in the tenth month. This time, it was also a princess. She couldn't hide her sadness.

Over the many years to come, Madam Gildae had more babies, and they were all princesses. Finally, it was the day on which she had the seventh princess. Madam Gildae felt so disappointed after she found out it was another girl. She burst out into crying that could be heard in Daemyeong Chamber, where King Ogu was. The king asked his servants to find out what the crying was. "What is this cry? What kind of a woman cries so that it reaches here? Please go and check." The court servants checked and found that it was the queen's cry. She was wailing over having another princess. They reported it to the king. "We are so sorry to tell you this, but it is the queen who cries in sadness after giving birth to the seventh princess."

With the news that it was another princess this time, the king felt even greater disappointment and became enraged. He said with a stern voice, "How dare the queen do this? How will she be able to look me in the eye? How much sin did I commit in my previous life such that God has appointed me with seven daughters? This child will ruin the country; please take her and throw her away."

Madam Gildae spoke, crying over this news. "Your Highness, you are so very cruel. Why do you ask them to discard a royal child?"

Madam Gildae, who could not abandon the newborn baby, asked the king whether it would be all right if the baby were sent to a servant without a child as an adoptee. The king became furious upon hearing her words. "There is no rule for adoption in this country. How can we give a royal child to my servant? Just dispose of her!"

After hearing the king in his towering rage, Madam Gildae summoned the court servants, gave them three shots of *eoju*,[4] and then asked to have her daughter sent away. It occurred to her that she needed to name the baby before she abandoned it. She delivered

---

4   *Eoju* is the drink that the king gives.

her request for a favor to the king, asking for a name to be given to the baby.

The angry king replied, "Normally an abandoned baby is called *beoridegi* and a discarded baby is called *deonjildegi*, so let's name her Princess Bari."

Once the abandoned seventh princess was named Princess Bari, Madam Gildae left her to the court servants and told them to send her away according to the king's order. The court servants came out of the palace as ordered, but they didn't know where to abandon the baby. When they laid the baby at the backyard where black magpies were flying, a blue crane and a white crane flew in and protected the baby with their wings. The cranes blocked the sunshine for the baby during the day and protected her from the humidity during the night, and the baby was kept safe and got along well.

After abandoning Princess Bari in accordance with the king's order, Madam Gildae wandered aimlessly as she could not stay well because of sadness and emptiness. One day, she went out to the backyard with the court ladies in order to divert her mind from sorrow. She then overheard a baby's cry. Madam Gildae asked, "What is this cry? Where does this baby's pitiful cry come from?"

The court ladies reported, "It is the cry of the deserted princess, who is hungry and misses her mother's arms."

Madam Gildae ordered, "Please carry the baby to my arms. Then bring a carpenter and ask him to make a box of jade."

The court ladies brought the baby to the queen's arms and called a carpenter to make a box of jade to give to the queen. Madam Gildae laid the baby in the jade box, pumped her breast milk into a jade bottle, and then gave the bottle wrapped around with a silk cloth to the baby, while covering the baby with a pretty cloth. She then closed the lid of the jade box. On the lid, she wrote with gold ink, "We offer the seventh princess of the king to the dragon king in the sea." The jade box was fastened with a lock with a golden turtle shape, but without a key. She then called court servants, gave them three shots of *eoju*, and let them carry the box, sending it outside the palace. Madam Gildae's heart was torn apart with the sorrow of sending away the princess, but she could not disobey the king's order.

The court servants who had been ordered by the queen did not know where to go. They carried the jade box and traveled deep into the mountains, where crows and magpies cried. After crossing one mountain range and then another, they reached the wide open sea. The sea looked bloody through their sad eyes. They couldn't help but throw the box to the sea, and a wave rose high and disappeared, swirling. A little later, the wave swirled again and rose up holding the jade box. Then the sea rose up again, and this time a golden turtle came out of the wave, took the jade box, and slowly entered the sea again. The court servants returned to the palace in grief.

In the meantime, the Buddha, residing in the Buddha's land, came out to the human world with his nine disciples in order to enjoy the spring days of March, when all the flowers start to bloom. At that time, a strong anima was surging and it surrounded the mountains. Clouds and fog then spread over the mountains during the day and an auspicious energy grew, emitting a light at night.

The Buddha asked his disciples, who accompanied him, "Dear Aranjonja and Mokryeonjonja, this must be a sign of someone that the heavens know, the heavenly person. Please go and find out what is happening."

The nine disciples looked around in the area the Buddha had pointed out, but couldn't find anything. They came back and reported, "In our view, there is nothing."

The Buddha said, "You are so far behind with your studies. Come back to me after studying again for seven years."

The Buddha sent his disciples out and he slowly moved toward the place emitting the auspicious energy, while holding a sutra in one hand and chanting the Tripitaka Koreana.[5] When he reached the place, unexpectedly, there was a jade box with a sacred glow. Looking at it carefully, he saw that there was golden writing on the top, "We offer the seventh princess to the dragon king in the sea."

The Buddha said, "If this baby had been born as a boy, I would take him as my student. This situation cannot be helped because it is a girl."

The Buddha put the jade box with the baby in the empty trunk of a tree. Meanwhile, Granny and Grandpa Birigongdeok, wearing string hats of the elderly, came down from the mountain and saw the Buddha. He asked, "Who are you people, wandering the mountain without any worry and with flowing snowy white hair?"

Granny Birigongdeok answered, "We are not ghosts or the

---

5 The Tripitaka Koreana refers to the earliest collection of Buddhist scriptures carved on over eighty thousand woodblocks.

heavenly gods, but the keepers of this mountain. Our names are Granny and Grandpa Birigongdeok."

The Buddha asked again, "Then… what is the best of human merits and virtues? Please answer."

Granny Birigongdeok replied, "It is to give a meal to a person who is hungry and water to a person who is thirsty. To give clothes to a person without clothes, to build a bridge over the deep river so that people can cross it, to spread grains on the luxuriant field, to build a temple in a high mountain… However, the best one is to feed a baby without milk and raise it."

"Then what about taking that baby over there crying for milk and raising her?"

"It is a great merit and virtue, but we do not have a house or a temple to stay in. We sleep in the field in spring and autumn, and stay in a cave for winter. We are grannies who beg for rice and wheat. How could we take that royal blood and raise it?"

The Buddha said, "If you take that baby and raise it, you will get something to eat, something to wear, and a place to live for free."

With that said, the Buddha disappeared. At last Granny and Grandpa Birigongdeok noticed that it was the Buddha's magic. They then looked at the box. On the top was written in golden ink, "We offer the seventh princess of the king to the dragon king in the sea." The box was fastened with a golden turtle shaped lock but without a key. They were flustered as they did not know how to open it, and they tried reciting the Tripitaka Koreana. Then, the golden turtle shaped lock clicked and opened. When they looked into the box, there was a baby, innocent and pure like jade. However, small thin snakes were covering her eyes; bubbles, her ears; sand grains, her mouth; and big ants, her entire body. They took the baby and washed her in running water, and they wrapped her with their Buddhist monk's robes that they were wearing. Suddenly, a straw thatched cottage appeared on which the Chinese character "王" (wang), meaning "king," was inscribed. They finally realized that it was the Buddha's magic. The two people lived in the cottage with the baby.

Time flowed on and on, and Princess Bari turned three years old, then five, and then seven. Without being taught, she came to know how to read and write and also realized the nature of life. One day, Princess Bari asked, "Grandma and Grandpa, all birds and animals have their mothers and fathers. Everything in the world already has a mother and a father. Where are my mother and father?"

"Grandpa is your father and Grandma is your mother."

"Please do not lie. How is it possible for old people like you with flowing grey hair to have a child?"

"That sky over there is your father and this land is your mother."

"Do not lie. How can the sky and the land bear a human?"

"I am so sorry, my dear baby. Granny and Grandpa Birigongdeok have committed a sin against you. We are old folks with grey hair who wanted to continue living life for you. However, we can't help that you are looking for your mother and father. Please go down to the yard and bow three times. The bamboo tree is your father and the grapevine in the back of the house is your mother."

"Please do not say such a ridiculous thing. How can natural trees bear a human?"

Granny and Grandpa Birigongdeok said, "This is not a lie. When a father passes away, for three years we wear a straw hair band and carry a stick that we cut cleanly from bamboo. This means the bamboo is like your father. When a mother dies, we must wear funeral garments and carry a stick that we cut from wild grapevine so that it has four edges. In this way, the grapevine is like your mother."

At last, Princess Bari trusted what they were saying. She visited the bamboo tree and the wild grapevine three times a day and took care of them, as she respected her parents. Granny and Grandpa Birigongdeok watched her with pity.

Time flowed on like water and Princess Bari turned fifteen years old. One day, as she prepared to wash her face, she saw the sun and the moon reflected in her washbowl and they looked far apart from each other. On that day, the queen fell seriously ill in King Ogu's palace. The king sent court maids and court ladies to Cheonha Palace to ask for a fortune. The shaman unfolded a red cloth, tossed grains of white rice, and selected the trigrams from the *Book of Changes*. Finally, the shaman opened her mouth as if she had figured out the God's will.

"The king and the queen are to pass away at the same time on the same day. However, if they can drink the medicinal water of Mujangseung, who lives beyond the land of death, they will return to life at the same time on the same day."

The court maids and ladies reported to the king what they had heard exactly as it had been said. The king summoned all his vassals and asked, "My dear vassals, who among you will cross the land of the dead, visit Mujangseung, and obtain the medicinal water?"

His vassals all bowed and replied, "In order to obtain the medicinal water, it is necessary to pass through the land of the dead. This is a place people cannot visit alive. How would we be able to go there?"

The king was very disappointed. He called the first princess, Byeolli, whom he loved the most and asked, "Dear Princess Byeolli, will you go and retrieve the medicinal water of Mujangseung for your father and mother?"

Princess Byeolli replied, "Dear Majesty, I am so sorry. This is a place where even three thousand court ladies cannot go. What would make it possible for me to go there? I am already married and my entire family depends on me. So I cannot go there."

The king became extremely disappointed with the first daughter, whom he relied on. Then he asked the second princess Heuk, who was cute and lovely. She said, "Dear Majesty, I am so sorry. How can I go to the place where even the eldest sister cannot go? I am supposed to visit my parents-in-law with my husband today. I cannot go there."

The King was let down again by the second daughter, but there was nothing he could do. Next, he asked the third Princess, Ok, who was smart and talented. She answered, "Dear Majesty, I am so sorry. How would I dare go to the place where my two elder sisters are unable to go? I am married and have a newborn baby, so I cannot go. I am sorry but I cannot obey your order."

The king was extremely broken hearted. However, there was

nothing he could do. The king called the fourth princess, the fifth, and the sixth in order and asked if they would go to find the medicinal water of Mujangseung. Each of them refused to go with their various excuses. The king fell into deep despair and sorrow. As his eyes filled with tears he dozed off. Right at that moment, in his dream, a little boy in green garments appeared in the yard in front of Daemyeong Chamber and said, "I am the boy in green garments who serves the Lord of the Heaven. Tomorrow, a guardian god, Geumgangyeoksa,[6] will visit you and take you to the hell called Pungdo-Jiok.[7] I have come here to tell you this."

The king was surprised and asked him, "What kind of sin have I committed that I am to be cast into Pungdo-Jiok? Do the government officials hold a grudge against me? Or is it that my people spite me? Or do court servants have a rancor against me?"

"This is not due to a grudge or rancor. The Lord of the Heaven blessed you with seven children, but you threw away the seventh princess. That is why the Lord is angry. Please search for her and find where she lives."

"Where in the world can I find my offspring, who I abandoned and left to die?"

"After traveling over a hundred million hills of hell, after passing the burnt hills, after traveling over the hill of prayers and across the Hwangcheon River, which one crosses after death, you will

---

6 Geumgangyeoksa is the god who holds the *Geumgangjeo* (a diamond stick) and protects the Buddhist law. This god stands at the sides of temple gates and plays the role of guardian.

7 Pungdo-Jiok is the hell where a biting, cold wind blows.

find a place called Seocheon. In that village, Granny and Grandpa Birigongdeok have been raising the princess. Please go and find her."

After opening his eyes in surprise, King Ogu realized that it was merely a dream. The king summoned all the government officials, court servants and maids, and court ladies. He announced that whoever found Princess Bari would receive a thousand pieces of gold, high official rank, and half the country as a reward. However, no one dared to volunteer. The palace remained in an oppressive silence and a torturous time elapsed.

Suddenly, an old officer stepped forward and carefully opened his mouth.

"Since my whole family has been indebted to the country from generation to generation by the allowances it has provided, I will go and find Princess Bari."

Upon hearing this, Madam Gildae became worried and asked the old officer, "Where can we find my abandoned child?"

"I reviewed the signs of nature last night. There is one place that is full of clouds and fog during the day and of auspicious energy during the night. This seems to be the place where she lives. I will go even if I am to die."

King Ogu asked, "What are you going to bring with you?"

"I will bring the things that Princess Bari used to use."

Upon hearing what the old servant said, the king was fully satisfied and gave him a drink to encourage him and to wish his safe return. The old vassal bowed to the king three times and exited the gate of the palace while carefully carrying Princess Bari's baby clothes. Even though he left the palace, he didn't know where to go at all. At that moment, a black magpie flew by and flapped its wings while looking back as if to guide him. The vassal followed it and went over many hills, crossed many creeks, and traveled deep into a mountainous area. He then saw a small thatched cottage where the character "王" (wang), meaning "king," was written. He joyfully knocked at the door. Granny and Grandpa Birigongdeok came out and asked, "Who are you? Are you a person or a ghost? This is a place where even birds or wild animals cannot come. How was it possible for you to get here?"

"I came here under the king's order to find Princess Bari."

Granny and Grandpa Birigongdeok said, "What kind of evidence did you bring that would lead you to recognize her as the royal descendant?"

The servant showed them the seventh princess Bari's baby clothes, which were folded carefully. Princess Bari, who overheard the story at the doorway, came out and said, "I have not seen this kind of clothing before. There are no babies without baby clothes. In what way do you know that these are mine? Also, even if there are too many royal descendants, why would they choose to desert a baby here deep in the middle of the mountains?"

The vassal kneeled in front of Princess Bari and explained the situation, crying all the while.

"To me, a single day is like ten days and a moment like three years. Please come with me quickly."

After hearing what he had said, Princess Bari put a patterned mat on the floor and placed on it a jade plate with a bowl of water drawn from the well early at dawn. Then she sat on her knees and held her two hands together saying, "If I am truly a royal descendant, the rain will pour down in areas more than ten miles away from here, but it will simply sprinkle within five miles of this area."

Immediately upon saying this, dark clouds began to cover the bright sunny sky, and thunder and lightning struck the world. Indeed, it started to pour in places more than ten miles away from where they were and to sprinkle in nearby places, within five miles. Finally, Princess Bari stood up and bowed toward the north where her father resided. She said, "The Heaven knows the moral laws. I will go to the palace."

The vassal was pleased and asked her, "Do you want a golden palanquin or a jade one?"

Princess Bari replied, "I have been living deep in a mountainous area, and so do not know of anything like that. I will walk there for myself."

The princess walked quickly and arrived at the palace. King Ogu and Madam Gildae shed tears, welcoming her, "Oh baby, my baby! You are Princess Bari. Come and sit here."

Princess Bari said, "How do you know that I am Princess Bari and that I am the one you have asked to come to Daemyeong Chamber? I cannot follow your command unless I confirm this by cutting my finger and seeing my blood."

Then the king asked the court maids and court ladies to bleed him by cutting his finger to identify if his blood was the same as Princess

Bari's. When they brought the jade plate, the king cut his thumb and Madam Gildae's index finger to make them bleed. Princess Bari cut her ring finger and compared her blood with the king's and the queen's. The blood ran in the same direction without spreading apart, and all of sudden, the clouds came out to bloom like flowers around them. The princess realized that she was royal blood. She burst into tears with a sorrow that had mounted over the years, and she bowed to King Ogu and Madam Gildae. The king opened his mouth without hiding his grief, "Oh, baby, baby! Please come here. I didn't abandon you for hatred. I was angry and imprudent. I am touching your head now, and it is cold and hard like iron. I am touching your hands, and they are tough and dry like leather. I am looking at your feet, and they are hard and rough like rock. How have you lived through the sweltering summer and how have you endured the freezing winter?"

"It was difficult in hot days and also in cold days. I ate grains in the field in May and June. I climbed a mountain and ate wild grapes and berries in September and October. It was hard to endure heat, cold, and hunger. However, the greatest sorrow was that I missed mother and father."

King Ogu asked the princess, "Now, we are in an urgent situation since the queen and I are sick. A shaman said that Mujangseung's medicinal water can save us. Can you bring that to us?"

"How can I travel a way that all six elder sisters refused to undertake? They were the ones who you raised with beautiful silk clothes of ninety-nine colors and with dainty nannies who fed them luxuriously. This is also the way that all the officials and court ladies refused to undertake. I did not receive any parental love that comes from raising a child. However, I was indebted to you for a night and to my mother for ten months inside her, so I cannot forget your kindness forever. I will go and return for my parents."

King Ogu said, "Oh, my dear daughter, you are admirable. Do you want military men or an excellent horse?"

"I do not need them. Instead, would you please give me a silk jacket and silk pants, an iron cane, and an iron topcoat, as well as a rough hat of iron braid and iron shoes?"

The king ordered them to be prepared quickly, and Princess Bari began to put on these outfits. She untied her long braided hair, tied a topknot with an iron hat, wore the silk jacket, hung the iron cane over her shoulder, and put on the iron shoes. Then she looked like a man. Princess Bari came out to the ancestral shrine of the royal family and said goodbye.

"After I leave, even if I do not return for nine years, please do not have funerals for the king and queen."

Princess Bari made this sincere request to her six elder sisters, all the officials in the court, the court ladies and maids. She then exited the palace gate and went on her way. Outside the gate, crows and magpies were waiting as if they wanted to guide the way and they welcomed the princess.

It was a spring day in March. There were yellow peonies, white peonies, azaleas, evergreen azaleas, and rhododendrons, splendidly in bloom. Junipers, cockscombs, orchids, and plants were also in full bloom. From the rocky cliffs, the sound of parrots and peacocks

preening their feathers could be heard from time to time.

Princess Bari hit the iron cane on the ground once and then she moved a thousand miles in one step. When she hit it twice, she could move two thousand miles in one step. Trees and plants were densely overgrown and the mountains appeared to be in layers and layers, while the water ran quietly. The crows and magpies guided the way to an entrance. As she entered, the Buddha and the Lord of the

Underworld (Jijang Bosal)[8] were playing Go (Asian chess) while facing each other. When she approached and bowed to them, the Buddha closed his eyes pretending not to recognize her, and the Lord of the Underworld asked her a question. "Who are you? Are you a human or a ghost? How could you come to this place, where even wild animals, birds, and blue hawks cannot cross over and reach?"

"I am the seventh prince of this country, and I started my journey in order to fulfill my filial duty. However, I have lost the way now. Dear Buddha, could you please guide me on which way to go?"

Hearing what she had said, the Buddha looked at her with his eyes slightly open and said, "I have heard that there is a seventh princess in this country, but not a seventh prince. I saved your life and yet you lie like this. You cannot avoid the hell Pungdo-Jiok if you deceive the Buddha."

"If the way to hell is a way to filial piety, I will go."

"Since your filial piety is great, I will show you the way to go. I will give you three flowers. On your long journey of three thousand miles to the medicinal water, carry these flowers in your arms and throw one when the wide open sea blocks you. The sea will then turn into a pond. When you cannot travel because of high mountains, throw this flower, and it will then turn into a flat field."

The Buddha gave three flowers to Princess Bari and disappeared. She bowed low with her gratitude and left holding three flowers in her hands.

---

8   Jijang Bosal is one of four principal bodhisattvas (Buddhist saints) in Buddhism.

Time flew on and on. It was difficult to count how many years had passed since Princess Bari had left. One day, she reached a huge, high mountain, where the wind and the clouds stopped to rest before passing over it. It was so high that even mature wild hawks and birds, and tamed hawks and birds, and eagles could not fly over it with their tired wings. It was the place where brambles and vines of arrowroots entangled together so that no one could enter or fly in. The Buddha's advice occurred to the princess, and she threw a flower. Then the high mountain became a flat field and the brambles disappeared.

After walking for a while, she reached a place surrounded by deep seas and surging waves, where she could not do anything herself to cross. Again this time, the princess took out a flower and threw it. Then the flower changed into a boat that carried Princess Bari, and she crossed the sea rapidly like a flying arrow. While flowing across the sea in the boat, she saw a castle of thorns and a castle of solid iron, which were so lofty that they almost touched the sky. In those castles, myriads of ghosts without arms, without legs, without eyes, and without tongues were clamoring and screaming in agony and appealing their pain. This was a place of torturous pain and appalling cries. These places were Dosan-Jiok,[9] Mugan-Jiok,[10] and Pungdo-Jiok, where various criminals were punished. Princess Bari asked, "How long are you to be kept here?"

The ghosts caught in the castles replied, "It is possible to be

---

9   Dosan-Jiok is the hell that is made of mountains of sharp knives.
10 Mugan-Jiok is the hell where people experience continuous pain as their skin is peeled off and they are burned in fire or where their eyes are hollowed out by a falcon.

released from here on the Buddha's birthday on April 8th or on *baekjoong* in July, which is the day of prayers for sending the dead to good places. If we are not released, however, we must be here for hundreds or thousands of years."

Princess Bari pitied them and wanted to save the criminals even if it delayed her in fulfilling her duty to filial piety. She threw a flower, and the thorn castle and the iron castle crashed down, opening the gates of hell. From there, the criminals without eyes, tongues, arms, or legs emerged. Princess Bari prayed for them all to be released from hell and to go to the heavenly world.

After the princess passed hell, she arrived at a place with a blue glass door on the east side, a white glass door on the west side, a red glass door on the south side, and a black glass door on the north side. In the middle of it all, there was a door of virtue with a man standing in it. The person was so tall that he appeared to reach the sky. He had a face as big as a plate; eyes as large as lamps; a nose that looked like a melon; ears, like straw sandals; hands, like the lid of a pot; and feet that were three *ja*[11] and three *chi*.[12] The princess was very scared and felt threatened. She stepped back but calmed down and then bowed three times to him. Then the man said, "Are you a human or a ghost? This is a place that neither birds nor wild animals can come to. How were you able to enter this place? Who are you?"

Princess Bari answered trembling with fear. "I am not a ghost, but

---

11 *Ja* is a unit measuring length (1 *ja* corresponds to 30.3cm).
12 *Chi* is a unit measuring length (1 *chi* corresponds to 3.0303cm).

a prince of the country. I came here to get Mujangseung's medicinal water in order to save my parents' life."

The man said, "I am that Mujangseung. Did you bring the money for wood, water, and fire?"

"I made haste in leaving, and so could not bring it."

"Then you need to gather firewood for three years, draw water for three years, and make a fire for three years. Then I will give you the medicinal water."

"If that is the way to save my parents, I will do that."

While working at gathering firewood for three years, Princess Bari's long silky hair became rough, entangled, and ugly to look at. While working at drawing water for three years, her fine dainty hands became rough and calloused. While spending three years making a fire, her pretty, fair face turned rough and dark. When the nine years of the promise had passed, Princess Bari talked to Mujangseung, "Please give me the medicinal water."

Then Mujangseung spoke to her, "You are pretending to be a man in front, but your appearance from the back shows that you are a woman. Please do not deceive me anymore. What about marrying me and giving me seven sons?"

"If that is the way to save my parents, I will do that."

Princess Bari and Mujangseung began to live together by taking the sky and the land as their house, thick clouds as the walls, grasses as their beddings, rotten wood trunks as their pillows, and sparkling stars from the sky as a lamp. She married Mujangseung and gave birth year after year to seven sons.

One day, Princess Bari had a dream. It was an ominous dream showing broken silver dishes and silver spoons and chopsticks. The princess woke up out of bed saying, "It is obvious that my mother and father have passed away at the same time. Since there is no more time, I must get the medicinal water and go back."

Then Mujangseung replied regretfully, "Please have a tour of the sea in front of the yard before going. Please take a tour of the flowers on the back hill before leaving."

"I do not have time for a boat tour and a flower tour."

Helplessly, Mujangseung said, "The water you draw in the front yard is the medicinal water that saves lives. The plants you have been cutting are *gaeancho*, herbs that cure blind eyes. The woods you have gathered are *byeokyiyong*, mysterious mushrooms for recovering senses and growing new skin if you put them into one's ear."

After quickly drawing the medicinal water, collecting *gaeancho*, and cutting *byeokyiyong*, the princess was about to leave. At that moment, Mujangseung said, "I lived alone before you came, but how can I survive by myself after you leave me? How can I raise seven sons? Take the children."

Princess Bari was about to leave by making the big kids walk and by carrying the younger ones in her arms and on her back. Then Mujangseung said, "If everyone leaves, how can I live alone? I will follow you."

"Ok, please do so."

Princess Bari left to find her way with her seven sons holding her hands and in her arms and on her back with Mujangseung following

her. When she had arrived at Mujangseung's place, she had been alone, but when she left, it was with nine family members.

When the princess and her family left the palace, the Hwangcheon River was running in front of them and a sea of blood was at their backs. On top of the river, boats were heading somewhere in a row. The first leading boat, skidding over the clear blue sea, was filled with blooms of water lilies, where chanting to Buddha was coming from. The princess asked, "What is that boat for?"

Then an answer resonated from the boat. "This is the boat for Yeonhwadae to carry people who have done so many wonderful things and charitable acts."

Looking at the other side, there were people colorfully decorated with various pieces of jewelry, blue tops, and red skirts. From there, resonant laughing could be heard. Princess Bari asked the boat, "What is that boat for?"

Then an answer came from the boat. "This boat carries to the heavenly world the people who dedicated themselves to the country, fulfilled filial piety, loved their siblings and shared happiness with family, and did so many good deeds."

The princess turned around and looked to her side behind her. Here there was a boat that was sailing, cleaving the waves of the sea tinted with blood. On top of the boat, people with handcuffs and fetters were hit with whips and were screaming in pain. The princess asked, "What is the boat with the noisy crying for?"

Then an answer came from the boat. "This boat carries people to hell. While they were alive, these people committed treachery to the country, disrespected parents, fought with siblings, created discord with family, threatened people into repaying many times the amount of an original debt after lending them some money, sold products by manipulating a scale, triggered fights between friends, stole others' belongings, slandered distinguished people out of jealousy, abandoned neighbors for greed, and performed all sorts of bad conduct."

When Princess Bari turned her eyes to the other direction, there was a boat with people with their hair disheveled and it was full of blood. She asked, "What is that boat for?"

Then an answer came from the boat. "This boat wanders around here and there with people who cannot receive a memorial service for ancestors because they are without any offspring and people who died in the middle of giving birth."

The princess and her family crossed the sea and arrived at the land. There, shepherd boys gathered and sang. While listening to their song, the princess caught her name. She carefully listened to the song and it was as follows:

Where has Princess Bari gone?
Where has the seventh princess gone?
Not knowing the nation's in mourning, she is not coming back, not coming back.

As she heard the lyric clearly, Princess Bari became surprised and asked the shepherd boys, "Boys, what kind of song is this? What do you mean that there is national mourning?"

The boys closed their mouths and did not reply at all. From among them, one said, "We cannot let you know for free. Pay the price for this information."

Princess Bari did not have any money, and so she had to give the silk cloth that tied the baby to her back. Then the boy answered, "Are you from the heaven? Or are you from the earth? How is it that you do not know the thing that everybody knows? The king and the queen passed away at the same time on the same day. There is the national mourning in the palace."

Startled Princess Bari hurried to enter the palace. However, she didn't know what to do with her seven sons and Mujangseung. She hid the seven sons in the bushes and asked Mujangseung to hide in the woods and not to move. Then she entered the palace without resting. As she watched the funeral march, "王" (wang) was clearly written for the king, and many servants were lined up holding *manjang*, the flag of sorrow with messages of mourning for the dead. The princess entered the palace in her haste shouting, "Please stop the parade of pallbearers with the coffins of the king and the queen. Dear court maids and ladies, please stand on the road, and all the officials, stand beside the road. The seventh princess, Princess Bari, has brought Mujangseung's medicinal water by crossing the land of the dead."

Then the pallbearer parade stopped. Princess Bari opened the coffins and poured the medicinal water into the king's and the queen's mouths. She put *gaeancho* on their eyes and *byeokyiyong* on their ears. Then, the king and the queen opened their eyes while breathing out deeply. They were resuscitated simultaneously. King Ogu cancelled the funeral order and gave an order for a king's honored arrival. The court maids and ladies wearing white funeral garments changed into green tops and red skirts and lined up to welcome the king and queen's arrival. They looked like beautiful flower beds. All officials removed their funeral garments and changed into official uniforms. Lining up together, they cheered for the king and the queen's resurrection. King Ogu called in Princess Bari. King Ogu and Madam Gildae shed tears admiring her.

"The princess we abandoned to die serves us this much... We are so sorry."

Then Princess Bari lay on her face and said, "I committed a sin. Without your approval, I married Mujangseung and have seven sons."

King Ogu said, "It is not your fault. It is my fault. By the way, where is my son-in-law, Mujangseung, and my grandchildren?"

"We came here all together."

"Please go to the son-in-law of the king, Mujangseung, and tell him to come."

The servants asked Princess Bari where Mujangseung was and brought him by themselves. Mujangseung wore the official uniform of the country and a coronet to meet the king formally. However, he was so tall that he couldn't come into the palace through the gates. All the officials reported to the king, "The son-in-law cannot come in because he is so tall, and the horns of the coronet get stuck at the door."

The king ordered, "Let him crash the door with a jade ax."

All the officials refused saying, "It is against a national law."

"Then, let him dig a tunnel and come in."

"This is also difficult."

"Then call strong men from the town and push him so that he goes over a wall of the palace and comes in."

All the officials executed the king's order and summoned strong men to help Mujangseung go over the wall. The king and the queen were quite shocked to see Mujangseung.

"Oh, my god! He is humongous. Dear servants, measure his height."

When the servants measured his height, Mujangseung was nine *ja* (one *ja* is about 30.3cm) and nine *chi* (one *chi* is about 3cm). Princess Bari was seven *ja* and seven *chi*. The king remarked, "You are a perfect match."

He asked them a question in order to keep his promise to Princess Bari. "Dear Princess Bari, since you saved your dead parents, do you want a high official position or lots of fortune or half the country?"

Princess Bari answered, "I do not want an official position or fortune or the country. Instead, please let Mujangseung collect the fee for when humans die and undergo their funeral service. Also, please take care of him by letting him receive the forty-nine day rites offered forty-nine days after a person dies. For my seven sons, please let them sit on Myeongbu Chamber in Chilseongdang, a place for the Great Dipper, the god guiding life, aging, disease, and death in every temple, when the forty-nine day rites are performed and take the money given for fortune and Buddha. Since Granny and Grandpa Birigongdeok graciously raised me, please let them receive ancestry worships on *hansik*[13] and *hangawi*.[14] Please arrange for the shepherd boy who informed me of the national mourning to receive a seven *ja* and seven *chi* silk towel. Also, because I became old without experiencing a luxurious life in the palace, please let me have a formal hairdo; hold a *samjichang* (three-pronged spear) and an *eonwoldo* (scimitar), as well as iron bells and a fan with fifty ribs; wear

---

13 *Hansik* is a traditional Korean holiday, the 105th day after the winter solstice.
14 *Hangawi* is a traditional Korean holiday similar to Thanksgiving Day, August 15th of the lunar calendar.

a wide red belt around my waist; and become a shaman who leads the dead to the heavenly way after death."

Since then, Princess Bari became a *mansin* (female shaman) who guides the way to the other world after death.

<u>Origin</u> Kim Jin-yeong & Hong Tae-han. 1997. *Collections of Princess Bari*. Vol.1, 2, Seoul: Minsokwon.

The song of Princess Bari is a narrative shamanic song that is sung during *ogu-gut*, a rite for leading the dead to an easy passage to the paradise. In this volume, the story was told based upon the actual narrative of the shamanic song.

Commentaries

Princess Bari, Deserted by People — Nonetheless Became a Goddess

Myth, Oral Tradition, and Repository of Folklore

The myth of Princess Bari is called the '*Baridegi* Myth'[1] and it belongs to the genre of narrative myths (a narrative song called by a shaman). Because a narrative myth is transmitted orally, its content is permitted to change as the performer changes.[2] In orally transmitted myths, traditional and popular conventions, custom, and thoughts are preserved, which is why myths become the subject of folklore research. Among the various myths, a myth about a figure shows how that person became a god or goddess. Now, how did a deserted

---

1   *Baridegi* means "a person abandoned." *Bari* means to be abandoned and *degi* is a label looking down on someone with a specific trait or property. *Baridegi*, so to speak, is a label underestimating an abandoned woman. However, because the main character's status is princess, the title of the literary work is "the Myth of Princess Bari."
2   However, the performer should not change the content related to gods because it is against divinity.

princess become the main character of a myth? This story shows a journey of a noble life in which a woman who was abandoned at birth survived struggling in her rough life's path and being reborn as a sacred being (a goddess). In line with this, her journey represents a traditional history of women's ordeals, where it embeds the power of mythological transmission.

Predominance of Man over Woman: "If it is a daughter again, desert her."

Princess Bari's father is King Ogu and her mother is Madam Gildae. When they were to be married, the lady of the court visited a shaman and asked her to select a good date for a wedding. The shaman predicted that they would have three princes if they were to marry in the following year, whereas they would have only princesses if they were to marry in that year. However, King Ogu rushed the wedding doubting the accuracy of the shaman's divination sign. He violated an oracle.

Madam Gildae became pregnant and had a mysterious dream. She told the dream to King Ogu, and he then ordered a lady of the court to figure out what the dream meant. The court lady paid a fee and asked for an interpretation of the dream from a shaman. The shaman read the fortunes and said that it was a conceptive dream (a precognitive dream about the birth of a child) and that they will have a princess. King Ogu did not believe this fortune because he hoped

Shin Yun-bok's *Munyeosinmu*. A shaman is performing a shaman dance to a tune played on a *janggu* (a Korean drum) and a *piri* (a Korean flute). The host of the shaman ritual (*gut*) is praying holding two hands together while putting rice on a small portable dining table.

to have a boy who could succeed him. This reflects a Korean way of thought, dominant for a long time, to value a man and neglect a woman.[3] In Korean traditional society, only a son could inherit the family blood and hold ancestral rituals (rites honoring the spirits of dead ancestors). For this reason, the culture of cherishing a son more than a daughter has continued, and daughters have been treated unkindly or ignored. They were even forced to sacrifice or hide their potential.[4]

---

3 The culture is connected to so-called *Namjonyeobi* (to value a man and neglect a woman) and *Namaseonho* (preference to a boy).

4 In Korea, some related lore has been transmitted. A representative story is a story of a brother and sister's strength competition. These days women's social status has become elevated while the birth rate has lowered, so the predominance of man over woman has been moderated.

Madam Gildae had six princesses one after another, and King Ogu was deeply disappointed. Finally, when the seventh daughter was born, his disappointment turned into fury. After all of this, he ordered the seventh daughter to be abandoned without even looking at her, and Princess Bari was left out in the backyard of the palace. Then a miraculous thing happened. In the backyard of the palace where only crows and magpies flew over, a white crane and a blue crane flew in and took care of Princess Bari in her swaddling clothes. This scene reflects the thought of respect for life, that nature does not abandon a person even if another person does so. As the baby cried from hunger, Madam Gildae ordered the princess to be put in a jade box and floated out to sea. This was because she was worried that King Ogu would find her out. In reality, it is almost impossible for a baby to survive alone in the sea. Thus, the queen wrote a letter to the dragon king in the sea with an earnest wish that the dragon king would take care of her. When the princess was thrown into the sea, a golden turtle appeared and went into the sea carrying the jade box.

Through the Abandoned Princess Bari, Asking a Way for a Human to Move Forward

It was the Buddha who first found Princess Bari. However, the Buddha gave up adopting her saying that he could not take a girl as his disciple. At that moment, Grandpa Birigongdeok appeared and the Buddha asked him what would be the best human merits and virtues. It was a question on the nature of humanity. Grandpa

Birigongdeok replied that it would be to give a meal to a person who is hungry and water to a person who is thirsty. He continued that it is to give clothes to a person without clothes, to build a bridge over the deep river so that people could cross it, to spread grains on the fertile field, and to build a temple in a high mountain.[5] This answer is common but proposes a way of ethical practice on how to act in order to live like a human.

In the end, Grandpa Birigongdeok answered that the best one would be to feed a baby who doesn't have milk and to raise it. This remark implies the philosophy among people that the real care is to provide people what they need and that this would be a natural duty. The Buddha predicted that if the Birigongdeok couple took the baby, they would be well off naturally. Although the Buddha did not take care of the princess, he helped Granny and Grandpa to do so. This symbolizes that the Buddha would provide if all living things were to chant a Buddhist prayer. It also shows that Buddhism was connected with people as a life philosophy that could be practiced in daily life instead of as a difficult philosophical ideology.[6]

Grandpa and Granny Birigongdeok received the jade box from the Buddha. However, the jade box was tightly locked, so they could

---

5   Birigongdeok's remark conveys that it is vital to take care of life, maintain a living through farming, build a bridge to connect communities and facilitate living, and build a temple as a method of training one's mind and disposition. These symbolize care, the way of symbiosis, and the method of civilization.

6   In fact, a philosophy of life presenting attitudes and directions to live as humans is widespread in Korean folk Buddhism. In Korean Buddhist temples, there are some cases embraced not only as Buddhist teachings but also as folk belief. Sansingak (mountain god hall) or Chilseonggak (hall for a God of the Big Dipper) are examples in which Buddhism embraced folk belief within the architectural structure.

Sansingak in Deogneung Village. Sansingak is related to worshipping mountains or village beliefs. It is an independent building inside a Buddhist temple. However, there are cases in which Sansingak was built in a village or a mountain and kept ancestral tablets. © The Academy of Korean Studies

Chilseonggak of the Buddhist Temple, the Unmun temple in Cheongdo Province. Chilseonggak is a hall keeping the god of the Big Dipper, who controls the life span. © J H LEE

not see the princess. When they chanted a Buddhist sutra, the lock automatically opened and there was a baby, innocent and pure like jade. However, the baby's whole body was wrapped by big ants, grains of sand, bubbles, and thin snakes. These symbolize the suffering of deserted Princess Bari. As they put the baby in the running water, she was washed clean. Then a house appeared in front of the poor couple. It was the reward from the Buddha for the couple who had conducted a good deed. They rendered thanks to the Buddha and lived along with the baby. This demonstrates that Buddhism was connected with people and played a role as ethical religion responding to the good deeds of humans.

"I will repay your grace to bring me to the world"

When Princess Bari turned seven years old, she started to ask about her personal history. She wanted to know about her identity. Granny and Grandpa Birigongdeok lied that the bamboo tree in the backyard was father and the grapevine was mother. This symbolizes that Princess Bari, who would become a god of the otherworld, grew up taking as her parents the tools that a chief mourner used (bamboo and grapevine).[7] In other words, the princess was disciplined since childhood for attitudes and qualities to become a god of the

---

7   In Korean traditional custom, if a father passed away, the child wore mourning clothes and walked with a bamboo cane for three years. Thus, the bamboo is father. If a mother died, the child walked with a grapevine cane. In turn, the grapevine is mother.

The Myth of Princess Bari

otherworld.

When the princess turned fifteen, unfortunate events happened in the palace. King Ogu fell seriously ill. A shaman read the fortune and predicted that he could live with the medicinal water of Mujangseung, who lived across the land of the dead. The vassals gathered together and discussed what to do; nobody wanted to go to Mujangseung. In order to go to Mujangseung, they had to pass the land of the dead, and above all they had to die first to pass over to the land of the dead.

Then King Ogu called his six loving daughters and asked if they could bring the medicinal water. The daughters told him with various excuses that they could not go. About that time, King Ogu had a dream in which a boy appeared and told him that he did not have many days left to go to the otherworld. He also added that since the king had deserted the seventh princess, the Lord of the Heaven was so angry that he had given him an illness. In order to save his life, the boy told him to find Princess Bari. The king called Princess Bari to the palace to save his life and asked if she could bring the medicinal water.

Gulgeon Jebok (Clothes that the chief mourner wears during the mourning period). *Gulgeon* refers to the thing the main mourner wears on top of the hood and *Jebok* means the mourning clothes. © Chonbuk National University Museum

Princess Bari said, "Those six

sisters who were raised in luxury cannot accomplish this. How is it possible for me, who grew up humble, to succeed? Even those excellent vassals refused to go, how could I?"

This remark was not one of modesty but a severe criticism. However, the princess spoke again.

"Because I was born into the world, I was indebted to father and mother. Now, I will pay them back. I will go."

She was delivering a message that parental grace is great enough with giving birth itself and the child's duty is to return the parental favor. For this reason, the abandoned princess left to find her way to death.

Hands of Mercy and the Path of Life:
Crossing the Land of the Dead to the Land of Humans

For her journey to find medicinal water, Princess Bari dressed in male attire. This is because it is dangerous in many ways for a woman to leave on a long journey alone. Through this, Princess Bari performed a male role as her social identity.[8]

During her journey Princess Bari saw various gods and ghosts. The Buddha who met Princess Bari when she was a baby was playing Go (Asian chess) with the Lord of the Underworld, Jijang Bosal

---

8 In Korean classic tales, there are many motifs in which a female protagonist disguises herself as a man when she goes outside her house. This means that a woman was not protected outside of the house. In parallel, it means that women could play a social role by practicing the code of social negotiation, i.e. dressing in male attire. However, this is not reality but fictional imagination.

(Ksitigarbha Bodhisattva). For humans, life was a rough journey but for gods, it was a simple journey of joy. Princess Bari left for her way again with flowers, symbolizing god's help. When she encountered a high mountain and brambles, they turned into a flat field. Then she met a deep sea with surging waves, which matched the customary expression of "life is a torturous sea."[9] The princess threw a flower and safely crossed the sea. She then encountered a castle of thorns and iron. She saw all sorts of ghosts floundering in pain.

That place was the hell where white ghosts were moaning in agony. The princess decided to save them even though it would then be too late to find the medicinal water. When she threw away the last flower, the door to the hell opened and all the criminals in the hell poured out. She prayed for them to go to heaven. Even for the criminals who had sinned in the human world, she tried to save them with generosity and love. The princess overcame the human limits and entered the way of a god by practicing compassion, love, sympathy, and generosity. In this process, Princess Bari met Mujangseung. He asked her to gather firewood for three years, to draw water for three years and to make fire for three years. Her beautiful face became rough while working hard. After nine years, Mujangseung told her to marry him and to have seven sons. The princess thought it was the only way to get the medicinal water, so she had no choice but to allow it to happen.

The period in which Princess Bari stayed with Mujangseung

---

9 "Torturous sea" means the world of torture and refers to the human world with endless pain. It is an expression referring to the human world in Buddhism.

Gamrowangdo (Nectar Ritual Painting) of the Seongju temple in Changwon describing the Buddhist hell © Cultural Heritage Administration

symbolizes married life. Her life was continuously tough labor. Moreover, she had to have sons and carry on Mujangseung's family line. Everything is far from Princess Bari's happiness and self-realization. On the other hand, it could be argued that Princess Bari's own identity and life were superseded by actions to maintain married life and family happiness. She accepted all the labor and sacrifice in order to acquire medicinal water to save her father's life. All the hardships Princess Bari went through were all with a mind for others.[10] The princess saved criminals in hell and endured tough labor to save her father.

The medicinal water Princess Bari desired to obtain was in Mujangseung's space. The plants and trees she used to cut were medicinal plants and the waters she drew every day were all

---

10 It refers to *itahaeng* (altruistic conduct), which is a Buddhist term referring to mind and behavior to give pleasure and eliminate suffering for others.

medicinal water. This also reflects sensibility and beliefs of ordinary people who viewed their current life positively and lived through it. Life is a place not somewhere far away but where we are living now. When Princess Bari first left to find her way, she was alone. However, when she came back home, she was with a family. Including her husband and seven sons, they were nine in total. On the way back home, the princess did not avoid ghosts in pain and bleeding people. Princess Bari led all the people and ghosts floundering in the otherworld to "the straightforward way."[11] This reflects that only a person in pain can understand and save others.

From a Human to a God: Self-Transcendence After Pain

When Princess Bari stepped on human land again, the first news she heard was about national mourning. Her father and mother had passed away. She hid Mujangseung and her sons in the bushes and entered the palace alone. She stopped the memorial parade for her dead parents and opened the coffins and administered the medicinal plants and water. Then, King Ogu and Madam Gildae were revived.

King Ogu sincerely apologized after his life was saved by the daughter he had deserted. Princess Bari confessed her sin to her parents; she had married without her parents' permission. The king, saying it was not the fault of the princess but his own fault, took

---

11 It means *jedo* (relief), which is a Buddhist term referring to leading all living beings to the hill of Nirvana.

Narratives about Origins and the World of Myths

Mujangseung as his son-in-law.

Mujangseung was too tall to walk into the palace gate like other people. This was because he was not a human but a god. A door is a symbolic device to connect or disconnect worlds. The act in which a god enters through a human door implies humanization of a god. Mujangseung was someone who had to live forever as a god. If he intended to come into the human door, he had to break the door. In the end, Mujangseung crossed over the wall and enter into the palace. As a god, he crossed the human boundary.

The king said, "Since you revived your dead parents, I will give a reward. What do you want?"

Princess Bari said, "I don't want an official position, fortune, or the country."

Princess Bari asked to become a god with Mujangseung and her seven sons. She especially wished to be a female shaman guiding the

A poster of the movie *Mansin*: *The Ten Thousand Spirits* (2013) The main protagonist of *mansin* (a female shaman) is Kim Geumhwa, who is a living shaman in South Korea.

way to the otherworld. In fact, Princess Bari was not a human but a god already. This is because she had crossed the sea of death and had been on a journey to the otherworld. In spite of that, she requested permission from the king to become a god because this showed respect for her father as a daughter. It was a message to reconcile with humans as a god. It also means that she wanted to become a communicator who negotiates and communicates with humans, but not a god who oppresses, dominates, and controls humans.

Finally, Princess Bari became a female shaman guiding one's last way, one who controlled death. Her life was a journey of ordeal. As soon as she was born, she was abandoned; she wandered the sea and grew up without knowing her parents. After she had grown up, she had to pass rough mountains, brambles, and the path to the otherworld to save her father's life and to find the medicinal water. However, when she came back to the land of humans, she grew up as an individual with the ability of problem solving and power. She became a god who saved people in torture, comforted dead spirits, and guided them to Heaven. She endured pain, took care of people in need, and trained herself to walk the path to divinity.

Instead of being crushed by the weight of agony, Princess Bari nobly sublimated that experience. She sympathized with others' agony and tried to save them. She freed herself from restraints and became a god because she found the way of purification and sublimation while overcoming her own limits. Thus, she was able to guide the way of the dead wandering on the way to the otherworld and to console those who lost someone they loved. At the end of pain, there is a way to self-transcendence crossing over life and death. The myth of Princess Bari was not buried in the way of suffering but accomplished as a sacred and divine narrative by becoming a god through *itahaeng* (altruistic mind and conduct).

Folk Customs in the Myth of Princess Bari: Conceptive Dream, Dream reading, and Morning Sickness

Princess Bari's shaman narrative belongs to a literary genre that has been orally transmitted. It contains people's direct and empirical life experiences and customs including a conceptive dream, dream interpretation, morning sickness, etc. Traditionally Koreans have recognized a precognitive dream about a baby's birth. Therefore, in Korean classic tales, the parents commonly have an auspicious dream before the main character is born. This contains the thought of respect for life in which the power of nature, stars, and the universe is involved in a human birth. This kind of imagination is passed down, so Koreans still talk about conceptive dreams and respect the meaning of them. In the myth of Princess Bari, there is a scene in which Madam Gildae, who had a conceptive dream, talked to her husband about that dream. It demonstrates a cultural custom that the story of a dream, a personal experience, is shared. Moreover, there is a scene for visiting a shaman to ask the meaning of a dream. People in the old days thought that dreams belonged to a mysterious area; they were symbolic and carried futuristic implications. For this reason, people visited a dream specialist (a shaman who plays that role in a myth). These mythological customs are transmitted to this day. Koreans considered a dream to be a sort of precognitive space predicting the future rather than an expression of unconsciousness or a suppressed expression of desire. That is why they sometimes talk about dreams to others and try to find their symbolic meaning. Even in modern society with advanced technology, dream interpretation attracts many people.[12]

There is another characteristic of an orally transmitted genre, that is, portraying life experiences dynamically. Consider the scene in which Madam Gildae experienced morning sickness, which included detailed description of changes in her body and senses. Morning sickness in Korean is called *ipdeot*. It is very rare to have such refined expressions on the change of the female body such as "felt her bones melting and her skeleton bending, while her bed was very uncomfortable" or the change in her senses describing "smelled uncooked rice from the steamed rice and smelled plants from the marinated vegetable." In those days, it was a cultural taboo to describe the change of a woman's private internal body. In Korean classic tales, the change of the female character's body or pain was not usually described in detail, and the process of delivery was fantastically mystified. However, the myth of Princess Bari contained ordinary people's sentiment by practically describing a pregnant woman's biological change. It formed a consensus among women that then spread publicly.

---

12 For example, dreams on passing an exam or lottery winning are widely shared.

Yeonohrang and Seonyeo

It was *jeongyunyeon*,[1] the year of the red rooster, the fourth year of the eighth king Adalla's reign in Silla. There by the eastern seashore lived a couple named Yeonohrang (a man) and Seonyeo (a woman). One day, Yeonoh was collecting seaweed from the sea, when suddenly a big rock appeared beneath him and carried him to Japan. (It has also been said that a fish carried him there.) The people in Japan said, "This person is an extraordinary man," and they took him as their king. (According to *Ilbonjegi* recorded as the history of Japan in *Samgukyusa*, this description must mean they took him as the head of a small village and not as a real king since no Silla person has ever been a king in Japan.)

Seo went to the seashore because she found it strange that her husband had not yet returned home. She saw the shoes that her husband had left then suddenly, a big rock appeared. When Seo climbed upon the rock, it also carried her to Japan. People in the country who saw Seo were surprised and found it strange, and so

---

1 *Jeongyunyeon* is the 34th year in the sexagenary cycle.

they took her to the king. In this way, the couple was reunited, and Yeonoh took Seo as the Queen Gwibi.

From that time on, the light of the sun and the moon disappeared from Silla. A fortuneteller who interprets the signs of the sky and predicts the future of the country said, "Before, the holy spirits of the sun and the moon filled our country. However, the spirits have

moved to Japan. This is the cause of this calamity."

The king sent a messenger to discover who had held the holy spirits of the sun and the moon in Silla. The king's messenger found that Yeonoh and Seo, who had been living by the eastern seashore, had disappeared at the same time as the lights. The king realized that Yeonoh and Seo had held the spirits and ordered that they be brought to him.

When the king's messenger went to bring them back from Japan, Yeonoh said, "It was the Heaven's decision to bring me to this country. How could I return now? Instead, my queen has woven a beautiful silk cloth. Bring that and hold a sacrificial rite to Heaven with it. Then, everything will return to normal."

Yeonoh handed the silk over to the messenger. The messenger returned to Silla and reported what he had heard. Following Yeonoh's instructions, they held the ritual, and the sun and the moon returned to normal. The king put the silk in the royal storage and made it a national treasure. The royal storage was called Gwibigo, and the place where the ritual was held was called Yeongilhyeon or Dogiya.

Origin Ilyeon, 'Yeonohrang and Seonyeo,' ⟨*Kee*⟩, *Samgukyusa*

Commentaries

The People are Heaven

A Metaphoric Device, 'Fantasy'

The story of *Yeonohrang and Seonyeo* is about a couple from the Silla dynasty who lived at the seashore. This story is in *Kee* of *Samgukyusa*. In the story, Yeonoh had been collecting seaweed when he is suddenly carried to Japan on a rock. Seo then also goes to Japan riding on a moving rock in order to find her husband. This is not a simple coincidence but an idea from fantasy. It is impossible for a rock to float over the sea and for people to cross from the coast of the Korean East Sea to Japan without any equipment. Also, it does not make sense that the couple went to Japan separately riding on a moving rock and were joined again. Moreover, how can we explain that the sun and the moon disappeared after Yeonoh and Seo settled down in Japan? It is possible to understand the story, however, by interpreting the fantastic elements in the text as a sort of metaphor.

Ordinary People are the Light and Treasure of a Country

When Yeonoh appeared in Japan riding on a rock, the Japanese people considered him to be an "extraordinary figure" and crowned him as a king. This was because he performed the impossible, something that an ordinary person cannot do. Yeonoh was a person with extraordinary power or a precious being protected by the Heaven. However, the Silla people had not recognized his true value because he led an ordinary life collecting seaweed.

The same was true for Seo. When she had been in Silla, she was an ordinary housewife. In actuality, she was also an extraordinary figure who could cross the sea on a moving rock. The Japanese people took her to the king and the couple was reunited. A common couple

A sculpture of Yeonohrang and Seonyeo (Haedoji Park in Youngil, Pohang, Gyeongsangbukdo Province) © Yonhap News

living in a village of the East Sea became the king and the queen of Japan. This implies criticism and satire of the Silla king, who never recognized the true value of his people. Right after Yeonoh and Seo left their hometown, the sun and the moon disappeared from Silla. This tells us that the ordinary people are the sun and the moon. The people are the light and treasure of the country. While living as citizens in the country, their value was not recognized. After they left, however, their precious value came to be known. Yeonoh and Seo were common laborers collecting seaweed in Silla. Those ordinary labors were the fundamental power sustaining Silla. In the end, the king sent his messenger to grasp the situation and he ordered the messenger to bring back Yeonoh and Seo.

Although Yeonoh and Seo were the Silla king's subjects, they became the king and the queen of Japan. Thus, Yeonoh responded to the Silla king's order as the king of Japan and not as a citizen of Silla. He then presented a solution for everyone with the affection and loyalty that he held as a former Silla person. He sent a silk cloth that Seo had woven back to Silla with the messenger. In order to weave fine silk, weft and warp need to cross in systematic order. Thus, the silk cloth implies the meaning of order, and the act of weaving mythologically symbolizes "order." When they held a heavenly ritual with Seo's silk, the sun and the moon magically started to shine again. The order of the universe was brought back in peace. The Silla king saved Seo's silk in the royal storage and labelled it a national treasure.

This story is short, yet it represents the spirit of humanity and conveys that people are treasures. As long as everyone carries out

A woman weaving silk cloth by crossing weft and warp.
© The Academy of Korean Studies

their duties, they shine like treasures of the sun and the moon. It is the king's role and it is good politics to recognize and acknowledge their value. Most people are not generous in acknowledging the true value of the person next to them. They miss someone after that person leaves and wish the person would come back. However, after they have left, it is difficult to change that person's mind. This story delivers the truth related to the value of people via an interesting fantasy.

A long time ago, astronomy was surely not developed to the extent it is these days. Thus, people may have been surprised at a lunar eclipse, when the shadow of the earth hides the moon, and at a solar eclipse, when the moon hides the sun by coming between the sun and the earth. Therefore, people may have considered a temporary disappearance of the sun and the moon as mysterious phenomena and felt scared. However, the beauty of the story is that the mystery was solved by discovering the value of ordinary people. Truth is always found in an ordinary place nearby. Since the old days, people with this "humanistic" creativity have lived in our land.

Stories of Love and Marriage

- Seodong and Princess Seonhwa
- The Idiot Ondal and Princess Pyeonggang
- Domi and His Wife

"You, my father, the King, always said that I must become Ondal's wife. Why would you change the words you said before? Even men in the street try not to lie. Why would someone with ultimate nobility like you lie? By the same reasoning, the king does not spit out ridiculous stuff. Your order is wrong, and so I dare to defy it."

Excerpted from 〈The Idiot Ondal and Princess Pyeonggang〉

When did you first feel that you were falling in love? Who was your first love? Even though you might feel shy talking about it with others, you probably have someone in mind and may have even thought that you would marry that person. Although in retrospect this love was simply youthful play, you may have thought at the time that it was serious. If so, what did people in the old days think about love and marriage? They also probably fell in love with each other and thought about getting married.

⟨Seodong and Princess Seonhwa⟩, ⟨The Idiot Ondal and Princess Pyeonggang⟩, and ⟨Domi and His Wife⟩ are stories about love and marriage. They are all married couples, but it is hard to know if they loved each other from the beginning. As you read these stories, think about them carefully. Did Seodong really love Princess Seonhwa? If so, at what point did he fall in love with her? If he loved her from the beginning, why did Seodong cause Princess Seonhwa's expulsion from the palace? When did Princess Pyeonggang decide to marry Idiot Ondal? If you consider the context in which she volunteered to marry him, that is, without meeting him, it may not have been possible for this to be a marriage between people in love. However, through reading these stories, we come to understand how two people who are strangers fall in love by being together.

The story about Domi and his wife provides a contrast in that it tells the story of a couple in love who is forced to lead a hard life. Through this story, we come to realize that marriage is not the accomplishment of love, but rather, that it can be another starting point. Moreover, we can understand that love and marriage are not just issues between a man and a woman, but also issues related to family and society, and furthermore, to a nation and the world. A joining of two individuals is a joining of one universe to another.

"Love and marriage" is something important, which people come to experience and encounter while living life. Therefore, the topic of love and marriage occupies a major part of all stories in the world, i.e. novels, movies, animation, and television dramas. These are stories about you, not about others, and for this reason, it is an issue that clearly requires serious thought.

The stories ⟨The Idiot Ondal and Princess Pyeonggang⟩ and ⟨Domi and His Wife⟩, which are introduced in this book, are listed in chapter *Yeoljeon* of *Samguksagi*. *Samguksagi* is the history book compiled in 1145 under the guidance of Kim Busik, who took his order from King Injong of Goryeo. *Yeoljeon* contains writings of various individuals' biographies, and it takes as its format a description of history through the life stories of "historic figures." People like Ondal and Domi belonged to a lower class, but they were considered worth mentioning in the history book and they remained in the record. It is worth examining in what respects they were acknowledged as you are reading their stories.

⟨Seodong and Princess Seonhwa⟩ is contained in *Kee* in *Samgukyusa*. *Samgukyusa* is the book that the Buddhist monk Ilyeon wrote by collecting stories of Goguryeo, Silla, and Baekje as well as Karakguk. Whereas *Samguksagi* contains a record of empirical historic events, *Samgukyusa* lists stories based on myths, legends, Buddhist narratives, and fantasies. *Samgukyusa* is composed of nine chapters: *Wangryeok*, *Kee*, *Heungbeop*, *Tapsang*, *Uihae*, *Sinju*, *Gamtong*, *Pieun*, and *Hyoseon*. *Wangryeok* is a chronology comparing periods in China, Silla, Goguryeo, Baekje, and Karakguk in order. *Kee* lists important historic events from the Three Kingdom period and lists fantastic and mysterious stories including myths, legends,

and folk tales. *Heungbeop* and *Uihae* list achievements of famous Buddhist monks. *Tapsang* contains legends related to temples, pagodas, and Buddhist statues. *Sinju* includes mysterious stories of a Buddhist sect and biographies of monks with supernatural powers. *Gamtong* has stories of associations with the Buddhist world including Buddha and Gwanseum Bosal (the Buddhist Goddess of Mercy). *Pieun* includes stories of hermit monks who were sequestered from the secular world. Because the writer, Ilyeon, was a monk, there are many stories related to Buddhism. The last chapter, *Hyoseon*, has stories of filial piety and good people.

If you are interested in stories from the Three Kingdom period[1] after reading the stories in this book, I would like to recommend that you read *Samgukyusa* written by Ilyeon. You will be able to read interesting and imaginative stories that deal philosophically with serious issues of humans and life, as well as history.

---

1 The Three Kingdoms include Baekje, Silla, and Goguryeo. The Three Kingdom period lasted from 57 BC to AD 668.

Seodong and Princess Seonhwa

The name of the 30th king in Baekje, King Mu, was Jang. His mother was a widow, and she lived in a house near a pond in the southern part of the capital city. She had a relationship with a dragon who lived in the pond, and she gave birth to a boy. The boy was called Seodong when he was young. Seodong was very thoughtful and incredibly mature. Because he earned a living by selling yams, people called him "Seodong" meaning a boy who picks up yams.

Seodong heard that King Jinpyeong's daughter in Silla was an unparalleled beauty, so he shaved his head and went to the capital of Silla. Since he generously handed out yams to children around the town, the children came close and listened intently to him. One day, Seodong wrote a children's song and asked them to sing. The lyric of the song was as follows:

Princess Seonhwa has a secret romance.
When night falls, she disappears with Seodong in her arms.

This children's song spread throughout the capital and reached the palace. The officials all urged the king to banish Princess Seonhwa to a remote place. When the princess was to leave, the queen gave her one *mal*[1] of gold and told her to use it for her journey. Princess Seonhwa left to find her way to her place of exile.

Along the way, someone approached her and bowed politely. She asked the man's name and he answered his name was Seodong. He then volunteered to accompany her. Although she didn't know where he came from, the princess felt safe and that she could trust him. She also felt peaceful and gratified. The two left for the journey together and fell in love with each other by the end. Later she realized that his name, Seodong, was the same as in the lyric of the children's song and that the prediction was accurate.

Seodong and Princess Seonhwa went to Baekje together. The princess was ready to live off the gold that her mother had given her. Looking at it, Seodong laughed and asked, "What is this for?"

The princess replied, "This is gold. With this much gold, we can enjoy a life of luxury for about a hundred years."

Then Seodong said, "Ever since I was young, there have been piles

---

1 *Mal* is a unit of measure (1 *mal* corresponds to 18 liter).

of these things where I picked up yams."

Princess Seonhwa said in surprise, "This is really a precious treasure of this world. If you know where that gold is, would you send these treasures to the palace where my parents live?"

Seodong answered, "Of course, let's do it."

So the couple collected gold and piled it up in a mound, but they didn't know how to send it. They decided to ask to Jimyeong Beopsa,[2] who was in a temple called Saja on Mt. Yonghwa, as to what they should do in order to send the gold to her parents.

Jimyeong Beopsa said, "I will be able to send it with my supernatural power. Please bring the gold here."

Princess Seonhwa wrote a letter and brought it with the gold to in front of the Saja temple. Jimyeong Beopsa moved the vast amount of gold to inside Silla palace in one night with his supernatural power. King Jinpyeong was amazed when he discovered that Seodong had sent an incredible amount of gold. Moreover, the king admired Seodong's extraordinary power. Starting from then, the king regularly sent a letter sending Seodong his regards. With this achievement, Seodong was highly recognized for his capabilities and he earned strong public support, which later allowed him to ascend to the throne.

One day, King Seodong was going to the Saja temple with Princess Seonhwa. As they approached the big pond down below Mt. Yonghwa, Mireuk Buddha (in Sanskrit Maitreya, a future Buddha of this world) suddenly appeared in the middle of the pond. The

---

2 Jimyeong Beopsa is a title for Buddhist monks.

couple stopped their cart and bowed in respect. The wife said to the king, "Please build a big temple here. It is my true wish."

The king promised to do so. He asked Jimyeong Beopsa how to change the pond into land to build a temple. The monk again used his supernatural power. He demolished the mountain overnight and created flat land by filling the pond with soil from the mountain.

The king asked him to make a statue of Mireuk Buddha by copying the figure he had met before. He also built a Buddhist sanctum, a pagoda, and an annex at each of three sites. He then decided the name of the temple would be "Mireuk" and asked to hang a board with its name. King Jinpyeong sent various skilled craftsmen to help. This temple remained until Goryeo period when Ilyeon wrote *Samgukyusa*. (In *Samguksagi*, Seodong was recorded as a son of King Beop. However, in *Samgukyusa*, he was recorded as a son of a widow. Thus, the truth is unknown.)

Origin   Ilyeon, 'King Mu,' ⟨*Kee*⟩, *Samkgukyusa*

Commentaries

Streets, Music, and the Cultural Politics of Children's Song

The Distorted Lyric from Seodong's Love Song

Seodongyo (Seodong's song) is the story of a nameless boy in Baekje who wrote a song and through that song, ultimately married a Silla princess. What kind of song did he write to accomplish having his love cross a national border and different social status?

The beginning goes like this: Seodong was a boy who made his living by collecting yams and selling them. The boy heard a rumor that Princess Seonhwa was an unparalleled beauty. He decided to go to the capital of Silla, Gyeongju, as he had a personal ambition to marry the princess. However, Seodong had only yams that he had lifted from the earth. Thus, he played a trick. He handed out his yams to the children in tow while singing a song. The lyric was extraordinary, saying that Princess Seonhwa was in love with him and meeting him every night. The message that the princess was secretly in love with a nameless boy from Baekje caused quite an unusual and sensational scandal.

Ultimately, the song that the children sang along to spread over the area and reached the king's ear. This put the king in a position of having to punish Princess Seonhwa, who had become the heroine of the disturbing rumor, in order to maintain the face of the Silla royal family. Otherwise, the ethical disciplines of Silla (rules and laws) were about to destroy them. It went against duty for the princess, who needed to serve as an exemplar to others, to be unmarried and yet to have a secret romance. On top of that, her partner was a nameless boy from Baekje, whose status was never suitable for her; so it was

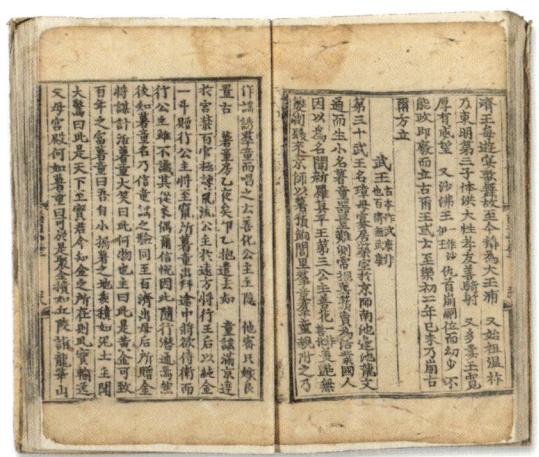

Seodong's song in *Samgukyusa*
Silla songs like Seodong's song are called *hyangga*. *Hyangga* were written using the *hangchal* system by borrowing the sound and meaning of Chinese characters. © Kyujanggak Institute for Korean Studies

a shameful scandal. The wave of gossip was too strong to identify the truth, and all the vassals argued for punishing the princess. The king had to tightly adhere to royal customs and to establish Silla ethics even if he had to punish his loving princess. Thus, he issued a declaration to send her far away from home.

The queen gave Princess Seonhwa a *mal* of gold, and when she was about to begin her journey of exile, someone appeared in front of her and asked to serve as her guard. Although she did not know who he was, she felt comfortable around him and he seemed dependable. The princess was tender-hearted due to her coddled upbringing. Thus, it was very natural for her to open her mind to a kind man when she first met him in such a strange and dangerous place.

Along the way they walked together, and they fell in love with each other. The boy's name turned out to be Seodong. Because of the false rumor involving someone named Seodong, the princess thought it was her destiny to be expelled and then to fall in love with the real Seodong. However, it was not her destiny. Everything was a trick made up by the Baekje boy Seodong, who used to pick up yams. If this was the case, was Seodong a swindler who spread a false rumor to satisfy his personal desire to marry a Silla princess?

Open Society and Ethics of Hope: Asking the Value of Humans in a Society with a Status System

Princess Seonhwa set up home with Seodong in his hometown of Baekje. The princess showed him the gold that her mother had given her, and with it, she said that they could enjoy a life of luxury for about a hundred years. Laughing loudly, Seodong responded there was so much of this where he picked up yams that it was like dirt. The princess was shocked; Seodong, who she had thought belonged to the lowest class, was actually a millionaire with piles of gold, as common as dirt. She thought this would give her an opportunity to introduce him honorably as her husband to her parents. She said to herself "If my parents know that Seodong is, in

A poster of the drama *Seodongyo* (SBS 2005-2006). A historical drama based upon the romance between Princess Seonhwa and Seodong.

fact, a millionaire, they will acknowledge our marriage and accept him as their son-in-law."

Seodong and Princess Seonhwa decided to send the gold, which was piled into a hill, to the Silla palace. However, transportation was a problem. In addition to the long distance, everything could turn out to be in vain if they lost the fortune to robbers along the way. They could even lose their lives. Seodong and Princess Seonhwa visited the Buddhist monk, Jimyeong Beopsa, to find a solution. Jimyeong Beopsa moved the gold to within the Silla palace in one night using his supernatural power. A handwritten letter from Princess Seonhwa was included with the gold. The king was surprised upon receiving the gold piles and the letter from Princess Seonhwa. Seodong turned out to be a man with enormous monetary power and capability. The king could not help but to open his heart and accept him as his son-in-law. He even had respect for Seodong because moving the golden hill in a night was not something that anyone could do. The king maintained a relationship with his daughter and son-in-law by exchanging personal letters. By gaining the king's trust through this event, Seodong later ascended the throne.

This story became a message of hope for people of low-class living in a society with a status system. Human value does not depend upon status or social position. The story contains the political message asserting 'Human value depends on personal capability, and Silla is an open society that recognizes and acknowledges this.'

Collaborating with Others and Politicizing Potential

It is true that Seodong belonged to the low class that picked up yams. However, he turned out to be a millionaire. The important thing is not that he was rich. Rather, the gold in the story refers not just to money; it also symbolizes precious value. People have precious value, but they need to find out what it is by themselves; their value can only be meaningful within society. At the beginning of the story, Seodong was introduced as a widow's son. It was because his mother had had relations with a dragon in a pond that Seodong was born. A dragon is a fantastic animal symbolizing something auspicious, and it normally represents a king. In other words, Seodong belonged to the low class and his father was unknown. Yet his unknown father could be a mysterious being with auspicious capability. The story delivers a message that human value should not be judged by appearances. Seodong was not the only one who recognized his value. He sent gold to the Silla king because Princess Seonhwa explained to him how precious the gold was. Therefore, he gained recognition in the society and became the king. Without Princess Seonhwa though, he may have grown up to be an unusual man singing well and picking up yams.

When two people recognize each other's value and collaborate, their powers multiply unimaginably. That is the power of collaboration and the value of the other. The other provides an unfamiliar perspective making the subject aware of things he or she cannot recognize alone. The other with an unfamiliar perspective is not something to be excluded, but a collaborative partner who creates synergy with the subject via communication and conversation. The collaborative pair of Seodong and Princess Seonhwa represents each collaboration of gender (man and woman), family (husband and wife), status (low class and high class), and nation (Baekje and Silla). Seodong's song demonstrates how collaboration with the other generates a positive power not only for the subject but also for the other and society, nation, and the world. (If you read Seodong's story again, you will recognize that Seodong was always with Princess Seonhwa whenever he needed a certain ability or a solution to a problem.)

After becoming king, Seodong maintains a relationship with Jimyeong Beopsa. Since Silla was a Buddhist society, the Buddhist monk represents not only a religious figure, but also someone with political and cultural impact. Thus, the part in which Seodong transports the gold to Silla with the help of Jimyeong Beopsa shows a narrative device in which he is able to negotiate with political and cultural power represented by Jimyeong Beopsa. Seodong was on the way somewhere with Princess Seonhwa when they happened to meet Mireuk Buddha (Maritreya); they built a temple and continued asking for help from Jimyeong Beopsa. The entire process implies that Seodong's political cultural power was supported by Buddhism, Silla's dominant ideology.

Seodong's song is a children's song sung by the children in town for fun. However, the song triggered many happenings. The princess crossed a border, a Baekje man and a Silla woman were married, and a low-class man became the king. A scandal became an admirable story, and a derogatory attitude changed to one of respect. The story also shows that a children's song has the power to change culture, politics, and history.

The Idiot Ondal and Princess Pyeonggang

Ondal was a person from the period of King Pyeonggang in Goguryeo. He was so ugly that others laughed at him, but he had an innocent and pure mind. His family was very poor, so he routinely supported his mother by begging for food. He always wore ragged clothes and worn-out shoes, and people called him "Idiot Ondal."

King Pyeonggang had a young daughter, who used to cry a lot. "With you crying all the time, it is very noisy. When you grow up, you won't be able to be the wife of a noble man. Therefore, I will need to arrange for you to marry Idiot Ondal."

The king always made this joke to his daughter. The princess grew up and turned sixteen years old. When the king tried to arrange for her to marry a man whose last name was Go in Sangbu, one of five major tribes in Goguryeo, the princess said, "You, my father, the King, always said that I must become Ondal's wife. Why would you change the words you said before? Even men in the street try not to lie. Why would someone with ultimate nobility like you lie? By the same reasoning, the king does not spit out ridiculous stuff. Your order is wrong, and so I dare to defy it."

The king became angry and shouted, "You dare not obey my order! Indeed, you cannot be my daughter. How could I live with you? You go wherever you want to go."

The princess left the palace by herself with dozens of valuable bracelets on her arms. Along the way, she asked where Ondal's house was and visited him directly. The house was old and shabby, and inhabited by a blind old lady. The princess recognized her as Ondal's mother and bowed to her politely. And then the princess asked where her son was. As the old mother could not see the princess, while groping around, she found the princess's hands; holding them, the old mother suddenly stepped back and said, "My son is poor and he is a no one. Someone noble like you would never come near him. I can smell your perfume and it is very fragrant. I also held your hands and they are so soft and smooth, like silk. You must be the noblest one in the world. Who tricked you into coming here? Out of unbearable hunger, my son went out to the mountain a while ago to get the bark of elm trees, but he hasn't yet returned."

The princess left the house to find him and reached the foot of the mountain. She then saw Ondal as he came down carrying the bark of elm trees on his back. The princess confessed what was in her mind. Ondal made a face and said, "This is not appropriate behavior for a young lady. You must not be a human, but a fox or a ghost. Please do not come near me."

Ondal ran away without even looking back. The princess returned to his house alone and slept under a twig gate. The next morning, she entered the house and talked to Ondal and his mother. She told them the details of her story, but Ondal hadn't yet made up his mind and hesitated. His mother said, "My son is just nothing, and as such, he is not worthy of becoming the spouse of an honorable person like you. We are so poor that it is not right for a noble person to live in my house."

The princess said, "There is an old saying, one *mal*[1] of grain is enough to pound in a mortar and one *ja*[2] of cloth is enough to sew. If our hearts are truly together as one, it is not right to say that we can only be together if there is wealth and fame."

The princess sold her gold bracelets and bought some rice paddies, a house, workers, cows and horses, and goods for the house; all the essentials of living were prepared for.

When the princess bought a horse for the first time, she told Ondal, "Please don't buy horses from market sellers. Instead, be sure to buy horses that belonged to the kingdom. They are ones being sold because they are sick and pale." Ondal followed what he heard. The princess fed them and raised them carefully, and they then gained weight and became quite healthy.

In Goguryeo, people used to gather at the hill of Nakrang every spring day of March 3rd to go hunting. They also performed rituals

---

1 *Mal* is a unit measuring amount. One *mal* corresponds to 18 liters.
2 *Ja* is a unit measuring length. One *ja* corresponds to 30.3cm.

for the gods in the heavens, mountains, and rivers, with wild boar and deer that they had hunted. On that day, the king joined in the hunting, and military officials and soldiers from five departments followed the king. Ondal followed them on a horse raised in his house. He was always at the head of the hunt on his horse. He also caught so many animals that no one could compete with him. The king called Ondal and asked his name. Upon hearing Ondal's name, he was surprised and thought that it was strange.

Around that time, the emperor Mu in Huju (a country in China that existed AD 907-960) sent troops to attack Yodong[3]. The king brought military men and fought against the enemy troops in the field of Baesan in Yodong. Ondal fought as a vanguard and cut off dozens of enemies' heads. Owing to his bravery, his troops fought with all their strength and won a battle with great spirit. Afterwards, when they discussed the exploits from the war, everyone praised Ondal's contribution as the best. With pleasure and admiration, the king said, "This is my son-in-law."

The king politely welcomed Ondal and graced him with the title of Daehyeong. From that time on, the king's favor and Ondal's honor were enhanced and his dignity and power increased.

When King Yeongyang, the 26th king of Goguryeo, ascended to the throne, Ondal said, "Silla took the north of the Han River from us and called it their province. Our people lament this bitterly and do not forget the land of their parents. Dear Majesty, if you do not

---

[3] Yodong is the northern part of the Korean peninsula (presentday Liaoyang).

think this foolish servant is unworthy and will give me soldiers, I will definitely take back our land."

The king granted his permission. On the day of his departure, Ondal swore to God, "I will not return until I take back Gyeriphyeon[4] and the west land of Jungnyeong as our land."

Finally, he departed for war and fought with Silla soldiers. However, he was shot with an arrow and died in a battle under the castle called Adan. When people tried to hold a funeral, the funeral bier would not move. The princess approached and said while touching his coffin, "It was already decided whether you were going to live or die. Oh dearest, please leave now."

Then the funeral bier moved and they could bury the coffin. The king was filled with deep sadness at the news.

Origin Kim Busik, 'Ondal,' ⟨*Yeoljeon*⟩, *Samguksagi*

---

4   Gyeriphyeon is present day Yeongju in Gyeongsangbukdo Province.

Commentaries

Cultural Politics of Sensibility Crossing Over Differences and Borders

Prototypical Korean Romance

The story of the Idiot Ondal and Princess Pyeonggang is entitled *Ondal* in *Yeoljeon* of *Samguksagi*. The original title includes neither Princess Pyeonggang nor the restrictive modifier idiot. However, this story is called "the Idiot Ondal and Princess Pyeonggang." What is the reason for this? The core word of the title is not the proper name Ondal or Pyeonggang. It is the status, idiot and princess. The story of marriage between the world's stupidest idiot and the princess with the highest status is itself interesting. This is because the story imagines crossing the border of different statuses.

Romance narratives crossing over differences are a deeply rooted tradition in Korean melodramas. The old Korean novel *Chunhyangjeon* portrays romance between *yangban* elite, Yidoryeong,

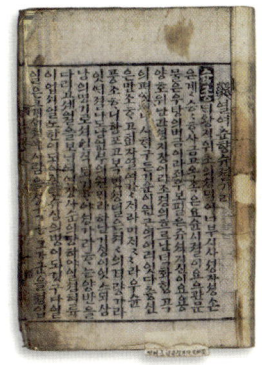

This is a block book printed in Jeonju, a version from 1911. The old novel *Chunhyangjeon*. It is a romance drama with a typical structure in which a couple overcomes a difference in status and marries. This novel also substantiates people's resistance against the social status hierarchy. It shows the cultural capacity and sensibility of ordinary people. Through satire and criticism against corrupt nobles, it demonstrates how ordinary people had intelligence and refinement equal to the noble *yangban* class.
© National Museum of Korea

and *gisaeng*,[1] Chunhyang. There are many modern dramas dealing with love between a man and a woman who overcome social status. For example, there are some Korean dramas. A *Boys over Flowers* (KBS2 2009) is a romance between a rich man and a working class woman, and another *Moon Embracing the Sun* (MBC 2012) deals with love between the Joseon King and a female shaman.

When it comes to romance, why do we imagine that people with different statuses come together? It is because the stories mirror reality, and they provide alternative worlds. In reality, people encounter many walls they cannot surpass. In the premodern period, it was codified social status and gender differences between male and female. Because of the advancement of democratic society in the modern period, society is no longer considered a status society. However, a material hierarchy triggered by capitalism still exists. Hierarchies exist in workplaces, organizations, and the military.

---

1   *Gisaeng* refers to a class of female entertainers for nobles and kings.

A poster of the drama *Boys Over Flowers* (KBS2 2009)
A romance drama in which an ordinary girl, Geum Jan-di, falls in love with a boy named Gu Jun-pyo, from a wealthy family. With its 32.9% top viewer rating, the drama was popular in South Korea and became so popular that it was recognized as one of the Korean wave dramas popular world-wide. The original story is based upon the Japanese comic book series and has been produced as a drama in Taiwan, Japan, and China, as well.

A poster of the drama *Moon Embracing the Sun* (MBC 2012)
This drama tells the story of romantic episodes between a king and a court lady.

The border or wall that appears between people depends on different periods, societies, and regions, and it takes various forms such as status, gender, age, generation, position, poverty, and wealth. The border does not disappear easily. Therefore, thought experiments in deconstructing the border continue to develop through the fictional genre of narration. It is because the wall in reality is so strong that people explore these issues through stories and enjoy imagining deconstructing the wall. The system that maintains the differences and creates the hierarchy is powerful. Thus, people thought the wall could be taken down by using their soft sensibilities to go between the spaces within the solid border. That is the romantic narrative. In Korean society, imagining deconstructing the border forms a cultural flow that criticizes society, introspects reality, and explores comfort and alternatives. This story is a success story of an individual; a Goguryeo hillbilly, idiot Ondal, married a noble and bright princess, became an outstanding general, and furthermore a hero by rendering distinguished service.

There is No Idiot: Esthetics of Meeting, Ideal Romance

The meeting of Pyeonggang and Ondal stemmed from her father, the king, and his joke. In order to make her stop crying, he teased her saying that she would end up marrying Ondal if she did not stop crying. This joke reflects the secular perspective on idiots. It is the perspective of despising and looking down on people who lack intelligence. The trouble was triggered as the princess then insisted on marrying Ondal when she was being forced to marry a man from a noble family. She argued that she should follow the king's word that was issued when she was young. The angry king expelled the princess; however, she never abandoned her will and she visited Ondal. This situation is very symbolic because her action demonstrated that even a king should not lie, even as a joke, and his promise should be kept once it was made. The princess showed that a king's trivial language and behavior should be politically correct. She also criticized her father, the king's attitude mocking and scorning one of his people. Even if Ondal was an idiot, he should be one to be respected.

In real life, Ondal was no longer called an idiot after he met with the princess. He was not born intellectually challenged. He had been poor with no opportunity for education. Because he lived in a mountainous area excluded from cultural life, he appeared to be an idiot. This was because of structural contradiction in society, not because of his incompetence. The fact that Ondal was called an idiot implies some criticism; it was not Ondal's personal defect, but the king's irresponsibility, as he did not govern the nation for his people to enjoy their life as humans and to be respected.

"You are not a human but clearly a fox or a ghost. Don't approach me!" This remark was made by Ondal when he first saw the princess visiting him. He did not believe that the noble princess would visit a poor young man in a mountainous village. This scene represents the reality of Ondal, who was pessimistic and had low self-esteem. It shows the sad reality of a young man who could not have a dream or an ambition because of poverty. Ondal's mother was the same. She was blind and could not see her. So she held the princess's hands and smelled them to identify who she was. Her soft hands and fragrance led the mother to feel far removed from her in her mind rather than to have a favorable impression. The mother put some distance between them saying that her son cannot be the spouse of the noble princess. Ondal and his mother's reactions demonstrate the deprivation and pessimism of others. However, the princess visited there and opened their minds, such that the borders of regions, status, and intelligence were demolished.

Political Power of Making a Hero: Lie, Trick, and Disguise

How was Ondal able to change from an idiot to a hero? It involves Princess Pyeonggang's sense of responsibility, wise tactics, education of her husband, and political power.

First, the princess married Ondal in order to correct her father's joke and turn it into a promise. She gave up the luxurious life guaranteed for a princess in order to recover the honor of the royal family. She left the palace, found Ondal in a mountain village, and accomplished her marriage.

Second, the princess educated Ondal as to how to buy an excellent horse. She knew that a horse looking weak in appearance could turn out to be a fast one. Her sense of horses exactly matched with her sense of humans. As she recognized the future hero in Ondal, she saw not the look, but the potential and possibility of the horse.

Third, the princess raised the sick horse to be healthy. This process is similar to the process changing idiot Ondal to a brave general. Ondal participated in the national hunt held annually and received recognition as the winner. He turned out to be a winner, not an idiot.

Fourth, Ondal made significant contributions to battles at the time of national crisis. As everyone acknowledged his contributions, the king declared Ondal his son-in-law. Ondal became a hero. This story delivers social motivation and expectation for the merit-based system. It also shows the power of social structure acknowledging outstanding individuals.

Behind Ondal's success, there were Princess Pyeonggang's wisdom, responsibility, leadership in guiding her husband, and enthusiasm for education. By keeping her promise, Princess Pyeonggang changed her father's attitude and rejuvenated Goguryeo as a country of hope. She also sent out a positive message: one's look is not everything, and even if someone looks stupid, she or he can be a hero by cultivating the capacity. The story shows all the processes of cultural politics practiced by honest Princess Pyeonggang, who kept a promise. Considering all this, we may question if she was really born an outstanding politician or strategist of that time.

True Esthetics of Love

What if Princess Pyeonggang was a capable politician who perpetrated tricks and accomplished her goals by disguise? If so, this story would not have been able to situate itself as one of the classics loved by people up to now. This is because people always desire for true love and support the narratives focusing on it. Pyeonggang and Ondal truly loved each other. The last scene of Ondal's death directly shows this. Ondal, who gained the king's trust, went into the war. He died honorably fighting against Silla troops. At his funeral, the coffin holding his body would not move. Although Ondal's body was dead, his sprit was not ready to accept his death. Then, Pyeonggang approached and said while touching his coffin:

"It was already decided whether you were going to live or die. Oh my dear, please leave now."

Pyeonggang's words are like those of a sage who is never bound with life and death. Ondal accepted his death in taking the advice of Pyeonggang, whom he loved and depended on. Pyeonggang was his mentor, who changed Ondal from an idiot to a general; his spiritual pillar; and a soul mate who shared his spirit. Ondal never forgot gratitude for his wife, who believed in his potential and advised him. Even in the form of the dead body, he expressed his strong trust in his loving wife in front of other people. Ondal and Pyeonggang's true love was the emotional esthetic power beautifully embracing social paradoxes, prejudices, and political strategies.

Domi and His Wife

Domi was a person from Baekje. Although he was listed as a commoner in the family registry, he was a man of honor. His wife was lovely and gorgeous. She was also known for her fidelity and integrity, and people praised her. King Gaeru heard about her fame and called Domi. The king said, "The most important virtues for a wife are chastity and innocence. However, there are few people who would not change their minds if they were lured by sweet words in a dark and desolate place."

Domi replied, "It is not easy to figure out what is in people's minds. However, my wife will not have two minds even in the face of death."

The king tried to test Domi's belief. He ordered him to work so that he could not return home. Next, the king had a servant dress in royal clothes and go to Domi's house at night on horseback. The servant informed Domi's wife of a visit from the king.

When the king visited Domi's wife, he told her, "I have heard of your beauty for a long time. Domi and I had a bet in which the

Domi and His Wife

winner would have you. I have now won. I will take you to the palace tomorrow as a court lady. You belong to me from now on."

With this remark, the king tried to treat her rudely. Domi's wife said, "My Majesty, I know you are truthful, so I cannot help but follow your order. Please go to the bedroom first. I will follow you after changing into new clothes."

Domi's wife dressed up her servant and sent her to the king. When the king realized that he had been deceived, he became furious. He blamed Domi for what had happened and had his eyes gouged out. Then the king ordered someone to drag Domi out, to put him on a small boat, and to set the boat afloat. The king pulled Domi's wife aside and brutally tried to force himself on her. Domi's wife said, "I have already lost my husband, and I cannot protect myself alone. I cannot avoid serving my Lord. However, I have my period, and so my body is not clean. If you wait for another day, I will come to you with a clean body."

The king trusted her and allowed her to leave. Domi's wife ran away immediately and reached the river's edge. However, she could not cross the river, and so she cried looking up to the sky. All of sudden, she saw a single boat coming down the river riding on the waves. She boarded the boat and reached an island called Cheonseong. There she met her husband, who was still alive. Because they had run away with nothing, they barely managed to feed themselves by picking the roots of plants. Since they would be killed by the king of Baekje if they were caught, they went to Goguryeo by boat and lived at the foot of a mountain. The Goguryeo people took pity on them after hearing their story.

Domi and his wife led a difficult life begging for clothes and food from the Goguryeo people. They lived out their lives as vagabonds in a foreign country.

<u>Origin</u> Kim Busik, 'Domi,' ⟨*Yeoljeon*⟩, *Samguksagi*

Commentaries

The Domi's Love and Trust

Samgang Oryun and *Samgang Haengsildo*

Koreans value the traditional virtues captured in *Samgang Oryun*. *Samgang*[1] refers to three fundamental principles of human life, and *Oryun*, to five moral principles. These principles are all related to ethical virtues of human relationships and are based upon Confucianism.[2] The moral relationships between king and subject, parent and child, and husband and wife are each included both in *Samgang* and in *Oryun*, although *Oryun* adds two additional relationships, one between adult and child and one between friends. Although *Samgang* simply mentions that each relationship has a

---

[1] *Samgang* refers to fundamental bonds between ruler and subject, father and son, and husband and wife.

[2] Here the term *Confucianism* is taken from a religious perspective based upon Confucius teachings. *Samgang Oryun* is its principal values and *Saseo Samgyung* (four books and three classics) are the Confucian scriptures.

particular moral discipline, *Oryun* presents more specific details. The five moral principles are presented as follows:

> *First, there should be justice and righteousness between king and subject.*
> *Second, there should be closeness between parent and child.*
> *Third, there should be differentiation between husband and wife.*
> *Fourth, there is to be order between adult and child.*
> *Five, there should be faith between friends.*

The fundamental moral values between king and subject, parent and child, and husband and wife are mentioned in both *Samgang* and *Oryun*. The moral education system is the foundation of a nation in Confucianism, and the moral principle between king and subject is mentioned first. However, given the family as the basic unit within a society, the principle of husband and wife and the principle of parent and child are more basic principles. When did Koreans adopt *Samgang Oryun* as the major principles of public education?

The Domi's story demonstrates that the ethics of *Samgang* were valued in the Three Kingdom period. The story appears in *Yeoljeon* of the historical text *Samguksagi*, which was compiled in the Goryeo period with the title *Domi*, and it appears in the section *Yeolnyeodo* (chastity women) of *Samgang Haengsildo*, which was compiled in the Joseon period with the title *Domi's wife scrounges for grass roots to eat*. (This book excerpted the story from *Samguksagi* and focused on the story of the couple because both husband and wife are the main characters.)

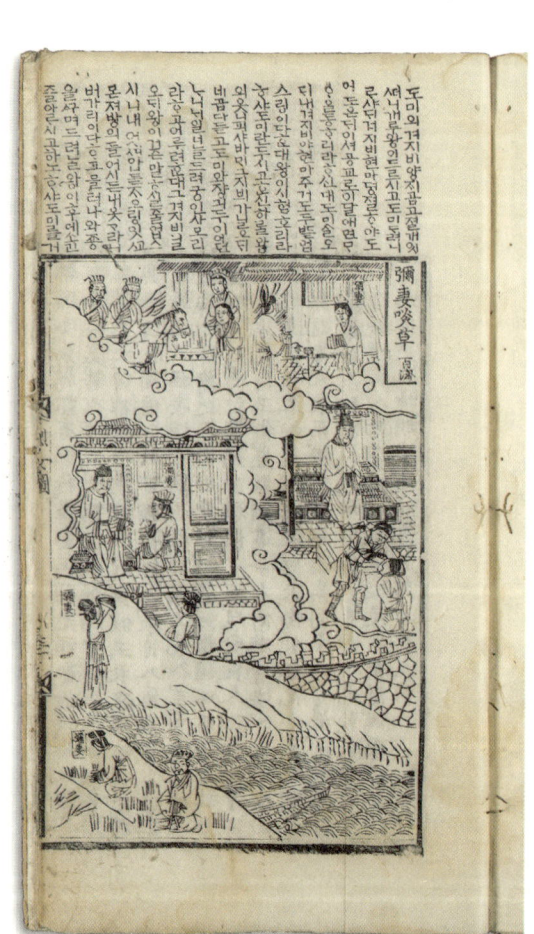

An illustration and writing of *Domi's wife scrounging for grass roots to eat*. In *Yeolnyeodo* in *Samgang Haengsildo*
© Kyujanggak Institute for Korean Studies

Domi and His Wife

Munjado (*Munja*: ideographs or characters, *Do*: painting). This is a painting in which characters are paired with symbolic objects; a story or folktale is connected with the meaning of the characters that are drawn in each stroke. The paintings were originally used as decorative panel screens at the royal palace or noble family houses. In the 19th C., *Munjado* in folk painting style became very popular among the people. The characters in the figures include *hyo* (filial piety), *shin* (trust), *chung* (loyalty), and *je* (brotherly love).

The Faith and Love between a Husband and a Wife

Domi was a commoner in Baekje. His wife was such a beautiful and virtuous woman, and people highly praised her chastity and fidelity. The King of Baekje, Gaeru, heard about Domi's wife and decided to seduce her. The king treated love and ethics lightly, like a game or a joke. He called Domi into the palace and shared what he was thinking. Domi, however, replied that his wife would never throw away her love for him. The king tried to shake Domi in his beliefs.

The king ordered his servant to put on the king's clothes and to go to Domi's house. The servant, accepting the king's order, disguised himself as the king and went and lied to Domi's wife

A portrait of Domi's wife (located in Madam Domi's shrine, Chungcheongnamdo Province, Korea) © Boryeong City

telling her that he (the king) and Domi had had a bet such that the winner would take Domi's wife as the prize. Because he had won, he said, she must go to the palace and become a courtesan. Then the servant in the king's clothes attempted to rape her. Domi's wife told the servant she would follow orders and she asked for a short time to prepare. She then dressed up her servant and sent her to the palace. As she had responded by mimicking the king's behavior, the king could not punish Domi's wife for her behavior. Nonetheless, the king became furious when his conduct was exposed, and so he caught Domi and denounced him. The king was a despot who acted with tyrannical authority and without self-reflection. Poor Domi was put in a boat, with his eyes gouged out, to float downriver.

Even after Domi's departure, the king's desire did not cease. He tried to seduce Domi's wife and rape her, but she escaped using her wits. She ran away and upon reaching a river bank, burst into tears having nowhere to go. Then like a miracle, a boat approached and carried her away. Domi's wife finally arrived at an island, and by another miracle, she met her husband there. When a miraculous event occurs, Koreans interpret it as a result of heaven's help. Traditionally, Koreans hold an ethical belief of nature that heaven never deserts people as long as they do their best with sincere intent.

The Domi's came together again as a couple on the island and barely subsisted, having to eat whatever grass roots they could scrounge up. They felt disenchanted with Baekje. The king of Baekje had desired a good commoner's wife and destroyed the husband's life. Leaving Baekje, the couple headed for Goguryeo. Because they did not want to live as people of Baekje ruled by a tyrant, they lived instead as strangers in Goguryeo drifting away from home.

This is a story in which the king oppressed his people and in the end expelled them. The king trampled on the love and firm belief of a good-hearted and loving couple. To the king, people were only possessions. However, the people thought that they could not live with their bodies and hearts imprisoned by power even if they had to subsist by eating only grass roots. 'Ethics' is a basic principle and a social promise to maintain humanity. The politics of tyrannical authority over humanity is not politics of reviving (life) but politics of destroying. The Domi's story highlights the value of ordinary life through the couple's struggle to keep their humanistic value in the name of love and trust.

Beautiful Person, Beautiful Mind

- Madam Suro
- The Filial Daughter Jieun

Dear Turtle, Dear Turtle,
Bring Suro back to us
What a sin it is to take away someone's wife!
If you do not listen to us,
We will catch you in a net and roast you for supper.

Excerpted from ⟨Madam Suro⟩

What is the most beautiful thing among all things to you, something so beautiful that you have wanted to share it with others? Several things might come to mind without any hesitation, perhaps something like winter scenery when white snows have covered the entire world. Sometimes your thoughts might be of scenery or a person. They might also be of your mother's bright face or of a note from your friend saying "I'm sorry" or of an unfashionable family photo from a part of your memory and so on. It could be of something like art work that you saw in a gallery or a fascinating scene from a movie or a firefighter saving someone from a fire or a person who has appeared in the news for donating a kidney to a coworker who needs a transplant.

If you stopped what you were doing and thought carefully, you must have realized that there are many beautiful things in existence, and as that occurred to you, you must have appreciated those beautiful things again. If so, let's imagine once more. This time, you are going to write down a list of things you feel they are beautiful and bury the list in the ground. A hundred years or thousand years later, someone digging in the ground trying to plant flowers will find your note. Is it possible for that person to understand the feelings you experienced upon reading your note? Instead of answering this question, please read the following two stories. These stories are about people who were considered beautiful in the old days. One story is about Madam Suro, who was famous for her beauty in the Silla period. The other is a story about a girl named Jieun, who although poor, was a filial daughter, and about a Silla *hwarang*,[1] who helped her.

After you read these stories and share in the feelings that were formerly held about idealized beauty, the contemporary beauty that you perceive nowadays can be thought of as beauty in the future. If something about the stories seems strange, it might be because the way of life, attitudes, or sensibilities about beauty from the old days have changed.

Come experience the old world with a curious mind, whether you think of it as beautiful or as strange. The classics provide the power to deepen one's thinking and broaden one's mind.

---

1 The term *"hwarang"* refers to an elite group of youths that existed during the Silla period.

Madam Suro

During the reign of King Seongdeok, the 33rd king of Silla, Sir Soonjeong was appointed governor of Gangneung (Myeongju in Goryeo Dynasty). On the way to fulfill Sir Soonjeong's post, the group had lunch near the seashore. Beside them, a rocky mountain cliff surrounded the sea like a screen as high as a thousand fathoms. At the top of the cliff was a royal azalea in full bloom. His wife looked at the blossoms and asked her servants, "Who will pick that flower for me?"

One servant said, "That is a spot that nobody can reach."

Everyone agreed with him. Yet, an old man guiding a cow had overheard what she had said. He picked the flower and brought it to her. In addition, he presented her with a song lyric. Nobody knew who he was. The song was called "Heonhwaga," meaning "a song for presenting a flower," and its lyric goes like this:

Near a purple boulder
You loosen my hands from a heifer.
Let me pick the flower to offer
If I don't embarrass you somehow.
Allow me to pick you a flower
If you are not ashamed of me.

On the second day, as Sir Soonjeong and Madam Suro were again en route, they had lunch in a place called Imhaejeong. Suddenly, a sea dragon appeared, kidnapped the madam, and dove back under the sea. Sir Soonjeong fell and sat on the ground. There was no way out of the situation. Then an old man appeared, "The people in the old days said that many people's tongues together melt iron. So, even if it is a sea animal, it will feel afraid of people's mouths. Please write a song and gather people here in this area so that they sing it together while tapping the ground with a stick. Then you will be able to find your wife."

Sir Soonjeong followed what the old man had said and called people and asked them to sing a song. Because they sang a song toward the sea, it was called "Haega." Its lyric goes like this:

Dear Turtle, Dear Turtle,
Bring Suro back to us
What a sin it is to take away someone's wife!
If you do not listen to us,
We will catch you in a net and roast you for supper.

When they sang the song, the dragon came out of the sea holding Madam Suro. Sir Soonjeong asked his wife about her experience beneath the sea. She replied, "There is a splendid and gorgeous place decorated with the seven treasures. Food is sweet, soft, fragrant, and very pure. It was not cooked in the human world."

Madam's clothes smelled good, but it was not the fragrance of the human world. Because Madam Suro was a beauty who compared to none, she was frequently caught by divine creatures whenever she passed deep mountains and broad waters.

<u>Origin</u>   Ilyeon, 'Madam Suro,' ⟨*Kee*⟩, *Samgukyusa*

Commentaries

Madam Suro, the Goddess of Beauty and Treasure of Silla

The Power of Beauty and Madam Suro's Attraction

The goddess of beauty appears as Aphrodite in Greek mythology and as Venus in Roman mythology. Aphrodite is adored as the goddess of the sea and good sailing, as well as the goddess of war. Moreover, she is the goddess of love, fecundity, and marriage. 'Aphro-' means 'bubbles' in Greek and the name Aphrodite originated from the legend that she was born out of white bubbles. Ever since Aphrodite has been worshipped as the goddess of beauty, many sculptors and painters have created works of art imagining her beauty. The *Venus de Milo* and Botticelli's *Birth of Venus* are representative examples.

There was a famous beauty in Silla, just like Aphrodite or Venus. She was the wife of Gangneung governor, Sir Soonjeong, and her name was Suro. Madam Suro was not a goddess, but a beautiful woman who possessed a mysterious charm. In fact, Madam Suro used to be kidnapped by mysterious beings whenever she passed by deep mountains or waters. She was so attractive that she captivated the god of the mountain and the god of the sea. After being kidnapped by the god of the sea, who was a dragon, Suro acquired a certain mystique like that of a goddess. She became a human goddess. There are two Silla songs related to Madam Suro. One is *Heonhwaga* (the song of offering a flower) and the other is *Haega* (the song of the sea). Both songs are connected to an episode that Sir Sunjeong encountered on the way to his appointed post, Gangneung.

Botticelli's *Birth of Venus*

A Song for Offering Flowers: An Old Man Becomes a Young One When Facing Love

Heonhwaga is the song that an old man sang after picking a flower from a cliff for Madam Suro. Suro was accompanying her husband who had been appointed as the governor of Gangneung. Suro, who was eating lunch at the seashore surrounded by rocky mountains that towered above her like a screen, discovered a royal azalea. She said, "Who will pick that flower for me?" Today the east coast of Gangwondo Province is still famous for its magnificent views.

In order to pick the flower, which was in bloom at the top of the mountain, a person had to assume great risk. Climbing the cliff itself was so hard that there was the possibility of falling to one's death. Thus, everyone declined the task saying that it would be too difficult. Then, a pedestrian—an old man passing by with a cow—picked the flower and gave it to her. He destroyed a common idea and a bias: that an old man would be weaker than a young man and would not have any interest in love.

Madam Suro's charm evoked from the old man greater courage and vitality than that of young men. In reality, it is hard to believe that an old man accomplished such a thing, and for this reason, some researchers understand the old man to be not a person but a god.

It's an important point that the story showed that the old man was attracted to the beautiful woman and fell in love with her. The old man sang a song while offering the flower, which makes it a love serenade. Faced with love, the old man was also a young one. This is the part where the subversive imagination of the Silla period stands out. Madam Suro's attraction crossed the boundaries of age and generation.

Chotdaebawi (Candle light rock) on the East Coast

A Song of the Sea: Beautiful Suro Cannot Be Taken Away by the God of the Sea

The sea dragon kidnapped Suro as her beauty captivated the god of the sea. Her husband Sir Soonjeong could not do anything in response. It was impossible for him to jump into the sea to save his wife. At that moment, an old man appeared and gave him an idea. He told him that people's tongues could melt even iron. Thus, if he called people and let them sing a song while striking a stick on the ground, he would be able to get his wife back. Sir Soonjeong followed the old man's instructions, and that song is called *Haega* (a song of the sea). The lyric was not about asking or begging for the god of the sea to return Suro. It was a threat (in which they called the dragon a turtle) to bring back Madam Suro. The lyric pointed out how wrong it is to take someone else's woman and it also threatened to roast the turtle for supper if Suro were not returned. The song was asking for a duel and it offered a punishment, all to save Suro. If the song were sung only by Sir Soonjeong, the lyric would not have been as powerful as it was. However, this song is a collective song sung by local people. Many of them sang the song, and together they were not afraid of the god of the sea. This demonstrates the power of collective sensibility that nothing is impossible if people unite and join together. Because they all sang the song and struck the ground with the stick, it must have shaken the earth. The sound of the group hitting the ground also shook the sea. Finally the dragon came out of the water and returned Madam Suro.

Madam Suro's Spell: The Person Who Experienced the World of Gods is Already a God

Sir Soonjeong must have hoped that Madam Suro would say she was so lucky to come back when she returned. He probably expected her to say that she felt cold and scared below the sea and was really miserable after being taken by the dragon. However, after her return, Madam Suro delivered an unexpected story. Beneath the sea was incomparably gorgeous and splendid; food had a great taste and aroma that is unimaginable in the human world. This means that the sea world of the dragon was mysteriously beautiful and was superior to the real world.

How did Madam Suro feel upon coming back to the human world after spending time in such a wonderful place? For whom were Sir Soonjeong's actions intended? While there was tension and conflict between the dragon and Sir Soonjeong, as well as between the dragon and the people, no one asked Madam Suro for her opinion. The charm of the story appears here. What was the world Madam Suro experienced? People thought it would be cold and rough under the sea, a space of death in which humans cannot breathe. On the contrary, people who had been there said it was a utopia. Madam Suro could have lived there forever. If so, however, human's desire and worry would have destroyed Madam Suro's happiness.

From the time that she visited the god's world under the sea, Madam Suro was not the same woman, one who was simply beautiful. Her clothes had a mysterious fragrance, and the smell

Madam Suro's Heonhwa park, Samcheok, Gangwon Province © Jung Yun-sung

implicates an authentic charm or aura that no one could imitate. A person who has experienced the mysterious world is no longer the same person as before. Suro is the goddess of empathy, communicating with the old man, the mountain god, and the sea god. The medium is Suro's beauty, which does not refer to a superficial beauty such as appearance. The true beauty of Madam Suro is internal maturity, a capacity to communicate, respect for a humble and old being's love, strong vital forces that are not weakened or destroyed, and understanding and tolerance that do not ignore the wishes of many people. The fact that these two songs have been conveyed up to now seems to send a historical message through literature warning us not to forget that sort of beauty.

The Filial Daughter Jieun

During the Silla period, there lived a woman in Hangibu village[1] who was the daughter of Yeon-gwon. Her filial piety was so admirable that everyone called her the filial daughter Jieun. The filial daughter Jieun lost her father when she was young, and she took care of her mother by herself. At thirty-two years of age, she was unmarried and never left her mother alone, checking her mother's health every morning and night. When there was no food left, she worked in someone's house or begged in order to get something to eat for her mother. Because of the never ending hardships in her life, she could no longer bear the exhaustion and misery.

One day she voluntarily sold herself to a rich family as a maid in exchange for a

---

1   Hangibu village is one of six major administrative districts in Silla.

dozen bags of rice. She worked all day and returned home late, after it became dark, to take care of her mother. Several days passed and her mother said to her daughter, "The rice before was so delicious even though it was rough. Now the rice seems to be good quality, but it does not have the same taste. I am in so much pain and my stomach aches as if someone has cut my belly with a knife. I wonder why that is."

The daughter confessed what she had been doing. Then her mother lamented, "I have made you someone's slave. This is no better than dying early."

With these words, her mother began to wail. The daughter started to cry too, and her crying could be heard outside in the street. The sadness of her crying touched people's hearts. At that moment, *hwarang*[2] Hyojongrang was passing by the house and happened to see the scene. He returned home, asked his parents for a hundred bags of grain and some clothing, and sent them to Jieun's house. He then re-paid the cost of the rice to the owner who had bought Jieun as a slave so that she could become a free commoner. Thousands of his fellow *hwarang* each added a bag of grain as well. The king (the 50th king of Silla, King Jeonggang) heard this news and gave her five hundred bags of grain and a house. He also endowed her with an exemption from public labor. In addition, the king was worried there might be someone who would threaten them or steal things from them given the abundance of food. Therefore, he sent an order to the government

---

2   *Hwarang* is a group of young elites that existed during the Silla period.

office and posted military men on sentry in turn. In order to honor Jieun's village, the king bestowed the name Hyoyangbang (meaning a village of filial piety) on it. He also sent a mark to the Royal House of the Tang Dynasty in order to celebrate the beauty of filial piety.

Hyojongrang was the son of Seo In-kyung, who belonged to the third rank of ministers, and Hyojongrang's childhood name was Hwadal. The king said, "Even though Hyojongrang is young, he seems to be very mature," and he arranged for Hyojongrang to marry a daughter of King Heongang, his brother.

<u>Origin</u> Kim Busik, 'The Filial Daughter Jieun,' 〈*Yeoljeon*〉, *Samguksagi*

Commentaries

Ethics of Filial Piety and Cultural Politics

True Filial Piety is Peace of Mind

This story of filial piety is a tale depicted in *Yeoljeon* in *Samguksagi*. The main character Jieun was the only daughter of a poor family in Silla. She lost her father when she was young and took care of her mother alone. She worked as a day laborer or sometimes begged in the street. Although she was over thirty two years old, she could not marry. This was because she was poor, but also because she could not let her mother stay alone. She could not escape from poverty in spite of her back-breaking hard work, and finally, she decided to

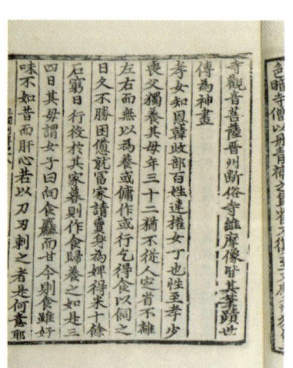

A part of *The Filial Daughter Jieun* in *Yeoljeon* of *Samguksagi*
© National Library of Korea

sell herself to a rich family as a slave. In return for working as a maid, she received a dozen bags of rice, which she served to her mother. Jieun's mother said the rice did not taste as sweet as it had before and her belly hurt as if she were stabbed by a knife. This was because good food was the painful price of her daughter's freedom. Her mother tasted the daughter's pain in the rice. When Jieun realized she could not lie anymore, she confessed that she had prepared the table in exchange for selling herself as a slave. Her mother wailed at the news that her daughter had been sold as a slave for her poor mother. Watching her mother crying bitterly, Jieun also burst into tears. Their wailing spread along the street.

Poverty and Misfortune, Ethics for Others, and National Welfare

Silla *hwarang*[1] Hyojongrang was on his way home when he heard the cries of the mother and daughter and figured out why they were crying. Upon returning back home, he informed his parents of this state of affairs and sent a hundred bags[2] of grains of rice and some clothing to Jieun's house. The price for which Jieun had sold

---

1 *Hwarang* was an elite training organization consisting of males from royal and noble families. In fact, it was an educational institute for noble male youths who were later brought up to be the leaders of Silla.

2 In the original text, the unit *seom* was used as a counting noun for bag. *Seom* was the Korean counting unit for grains, powder, or liquor. One *seom* is equivalent to 10 *mal* and it corresponds to 180 liters.

herself was only a dozen bags of rice, but Hyojongrang had given her a hundred bags. This demonstrates how terrible the plight of poor people was at that time and also how generous Hyojongrang's benevolence was. He repaid the owner who had bought Jieun as a maid and set her free. He did not look on the misfortune of others, but actively became involved in solving their problems. Once Hyojongrang's good deed became public, thousands of his fellow *hwarang* emulated the conduct of their leader, Hyojongrang, each sending a bag of rice. The king also heard the news and granted Hyojongrang various benefits. In addition, he bestowed the name Hyoyangbang (meaning village of filial piety) to praise the village of the filial daughter.

Filial piety was the ethic that the country promoted. Moreover, the king informed the Royal House of Tang of this fact in order to announce the beautiful culture of Silla to the world and to invite them to share in it together. The king highly valued Hyojongrang, who paid attention to the unhappiness of common people and actively helped them. Thus, the king arranged for Hyojongrang to marry the daughter of King Heongang, his elder brother. Through his benevolent act, Hyojongrang's status was promoted from a noble man to a royal family member.

The filial daughter Jieun's story does more than convey the ethical value of maintaining filial piety regardless of hardship. This story emphasizes several different aspects of filial piety. First, filial piety is a precious ethical value that every individual needs to maintain. Second, it is an ethical value of society. This ethical value needs to be respected within a family not only by family members, but it is also the concern of a community living together. Thus, it is a social ethic. Third, a nation needs to help keep individual, familial, and societal ethics in harmony. Fourth, filial piety is an ethical value that is not limited only to the levels of individuals, society, and nation, but at the world level, it should be globally sympathized and respected.

Social Practices of *hwarang*, the Duty and Roles of the Leadership, and Harmonious Silla Society

Although the main character of this story is the filial daughter Jieun, the next young leader Hyojongrang also deserves mention. He was the leader of thousands of *hwarang*. He paid attention to the wailing sound that he heard accidentally in the street and gave of his personal

A scene of *hwarang* training in the drama *Queen Seondeok* (The man standing in front of the other men in rows and leading them is Kim Yu-sin, who played an important role in unifying the three kingdoms).

assets. He was a leader who was attentive to the unhappiness of others and took good care of them instead of passing by or ignoring them. As thousands of his fellow *hwarang* each provided a bag of rice, Jieun came to possess thousands of bags. The ethic of *sipsiilban*, 'Ten spoons of rice become a bowl',[3] was practiced. The king who was informed of Hyojongrang's good act, awarded him a prize and praised him, and took him into the royal family.

Silla was a society with a status system. Therefore, a person born to nobility became a noble and a member of the leadership class. On the one hand, this story emphasizes how a person born into a leadership position did not tyrannize others and misuse authority, but grew into a qualified leader and fulfilled actions of social practice. In addition, it sends the message that the nation observed these behaviors and acknowledged good conduct. The story was used as a medium of cultural politics advertising that the *hwarang* youth organization paid keen attention to every part of Silla society and nurtured their qualifications as the next leaders.

On the other hand, the story implies that the king conducted politics according to people's ethical practices at the national level and that Silla's status system was reasonable and right. It also shows the national pride that Silla held in a having peaceful, harmonious relationships with the world while sharing that a

---

3 *Sipsiilban* meaning 'each spoon makes a bowl of rice' suggests that it becomes easier to help a person when several people cooperate a little. The culture of *sipsiilban* can be found in Korea nowadays as well. A representative example is when citizens as a whole collect funds to help victims of disasters.

poor girl's behavior was known to the Royal House of Tang and acknowledged by them.

The World of Fantasy

- Josin's Dream
- *Kim Hyeon Gam Ho*
- *Yi Saeng Gyu Jang Jeon*

At the moment the two said goodbye and were about to leave, Josin woke up from his dream. Under the dimming oil lamp, the night had become deeper and deeper. When morning broke, his hair and beard had turned completely white, and he had lost all will to live.

Excerpted from ⟨Josin's Dream⟩

In literature, "fantasy" is a mysterious story describing events not seen in this world, but believed to exist in an imaginary world that is unreal, transcendental, and scientifically inexplicable. For example, there are stories that show an imaginary world with its own unique order in the narrative space; even though that world is not real, such stories of ghosts, adventure to the world of the dead, and travel across the universe repeatedly evolve. The world of fantastic literature originates from myths that initially appear in the history of narratives. Gods including Jumong's father, Haemosu; the god of rivers, Habaek; and Princess Bari, who guides the way to death, are fantastic beings. Likewise, "fantasy" has always been an element of narratives from the start.

Why do people like the world of fantasy? What kinds of things do people experience in these artificial worlds that do not really exist, but feel as if they are real? In the fantasy world, an independent world appears that is distinct from reality. That world is represented as a perfect ideal world without contradiction or negative elements, or as an imperfect world, but one dominated by principles that differ from those in the real world. Sometimes it is represented as a world that is similar to the real one. These kinds of fantasy worlds are attractive in that they demonstrate incredible imaginary powers, and in some respects, they are useful tools that lead us to reflect on the real world in which we live.

Three stories in this chapter each include fantasy worlds. In ⟨Josin's Dream⟩, the story deals with the process by which a monk named Josin realizes the emptiness of life and the vanity of desire through travel in his dreams. ⟨The Love between Kim Hyeon and a Lady Tiger⟩ chases the meaning of true love and of being human though the unrealistic love story between a human and a tiger with the power to transform into a human. ⟨The Story of Yi Saeng Peering over the Wall⟩ is a story in which a woman who dies in a war comes back as a ghost and completes her unfinished love. Although love between a ghost and a human is impossible in the real world, by assuming a fantasy world, the story is able to deal with the tragic reality of an individual who was only allowed to live as a ghost. The fantasy worlds in these stories are all artificial worlds presented as a way to reflect on reality. In former times, people thought about reality through fantasy and pursued the virtue of humanism.

Josin's Dream

A long time ago, when Seorabeol was the capital of Silla, there was a Buddhist temple called Segyu. The temple managed land in Nalli-gun in Myeongju,[1] and it sent a monk named Josin to take care of the land. Josin stayed there and lost his heart to Governor Kim Heungong's daughter. He prayed to the Buddhist Goddess of Mercy to make his love for her come true. However, in a few years, she married another man.

Josin went to the Goddess of Mercy and reproached her. He cried and cried. Darkness fell, but his love didn't falter. He became tired from crying and shortly fell asleep. Suddenly, Lady Kim, the Governor's daughter, appeared in his dream. She entered pleasantly through a door and said with a big smile, "I saw you briefly, a while ago, and fell in love with you. Since that time, I have never forgotten you. However, as I could not go against my parents' orders, I have had to marry someone else. Still, I wish to join with you as a couple,

---

[1] Myeongju is one of the administrative districts in Silla and Goryeo, which corresponds to the city, Gangneung today.

and so I have come down to you like this."

Josin was so happy that he returned to his hometown with the lady. They lived together for forty years and had five children. However, his house had nothing, just walls. They could barely afford food. Because they were extremely poor, his family had to go around begging and could barely make a living. They lived this way as another ten years passed. As they moved from field to field, their clothes became torn and could no longer cover their bodies. While they were passing the hill called Haehyeonryeong in Myeongju, the first child, who was 15 years old, died suddenly from hunger. Josin wailed and buried the body by the roadside. Carrying the four remaining children, they reached the village named Ugokhyeon and built a thatched cottage near the street. The couple was so old and sick that they didn't even have the energy to stand.

One day, the ten-year-old daughter went out begging and was bitten by a dog in town. The daughter came back home crying out in pain and collapsed in front of the couple. They sobbed becoming drenched with tears. The wife choked up from crying and said to her husband while wiping her tears, "When I met you for the first time, I was beautiful and young like a flower. I wore good clothes and I was clean. If I had something delicious,

I shared it with you. Even if the things I had were shabby, I shared everything with you. It has been more than fifty years since I left my home. We have built a deep emotional connection and strengthened our love, and these are seen as strong bonds. However, these days, I am growing weak and worse from illness.

In addition, the starvation and cold are even more severe, yet people do not shelter us and refuse to give us even a bottle of soybean sauce. My embarrassment in front of people is as heavy as mountains. I can do nothing to help even though the children are tortured with cold and hunger. How can we share our love in a situation like this? The beautiful smile on my peach colored face has disappeared like the morning dew on plants, and our sincere promises have blown away like willows in the wind. I have become a burden on you and you have become my worry. Looking back at all the pleasures from the old days, everything was the beginning of worry and anxiety. How did we reach a situation like this? Rather than both birds dying from hunger, it is better that one bird lament missing a mate. It is not humane to abandon each other in need and to stay together in good situations. However, humans can do nothing to make things happen or not happen. Separating or meeting depends on destiny. Please, listen to what I say."

As Josin was also worn out, he began to take comfort and satisfaction in hearing her remarks. He suggested that each of them take two children and part ways. The wife said, "I will go back to my hometown. You go to the south."

At the moment the two said goodbye and were about to leave,

Josin's Dream

Josin woke up from his dream. Under the dimming oil lamp, the night had become deeper and deeper. When the morning broke, his hair and beard had turned completely white, and he had lost all will to live. He felt so tired of living as if he had gone through a hundred years of pain. His desire had completely disappeared. He couldn't even dare to look at the Goddess of Mercy in shame. Josin repented again and again.

Josin went to Haehyeon, and where he had buried his child in his dream, there was a stone statue of Buddha. He washed it and worshipped it in a neighboring temple. After returning to the capital, he quit his position as a manager of a manor and built a Buddhist temple called Jeongto using the entirety of his private fortune. After that, he put all his energy into doing good things, but it is unknown when he died.

I, the narrator of this story (Ilyeon), wrote a poem to explain why I have included this story.

"After reading this story and thinking back upon the past, I realize that our life is like Josin's dream. These days, people only enjoy and pursue secular pleasures. This is because they don't realize that life is like a dream. Thus, I wrote the following poem as a warning:

For a short while, as I felt refreshed and happy
My mind became quiet and calm
But all along I aged in secret with worries.

Without even waiting for a bowl of cooked millet[2]
I realize that the whole of my life was just a dream.
Training the mind is said to be destiny
But a thief still dreams of full bounty and a widower a beautiful woman.
Here in the autumn of my days
Will I be able to close my eyes on a clear night
And by dreaming, arrive at a state of clarity?

<u>Origin</u> Ilyeon, 'Naksanidaeseong, Gwaneum, Jeongchwi, Josin,' ⟨Tapsang⟩, *Samgukyusa*

---

2 *Without even waiting for a bowl of cooked millet*: In the Tang Dynasty in China, a young lad named Nohsaeng fell asleep in a local tavern, and in his dream, he enjoyed a luxurious life until he was 80 years old. When he woke up, it was still before the millet at the tavern had been cooked. The expression comes from this story and suggests that wealth and fame are in vain.

Commentaries

Josin's Dream, Introspective Reflection of Desire

Life is like a Dream

Josin's dream is a story in *Samgukyusa*. The story reflects the traditional Asian way of thinking that life is like a dream. This way of thinking is rooted in the philosophical foundation of the Buddhist concept of *gong* (Sanskrit, Śūnyatā; emptiness or void in English). According to the concept of *gong*, everything is, in fact, empty, as it has never existed before, nor has it not existed. This concept involves being cautious of realistic and materialistic greed, and examining reality

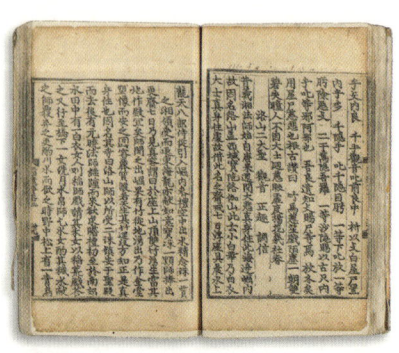

Josin's dream, Original texts of
'Naksanidaeseong Gwaneum, Jeongchwi, Josin,' *Tapsang* in *Samgukyusa*
© Kyujanggak Institute for Korean Studies

and the origins of being.

Everyone has goals and dreams in life. In other words, people have what they want to accomplish or the state of being in which they want to be. In order to achieve these goals, they give up other things or restrain themselves. People tend to praise this as passion for a dream. When people reach their goals, they again ask new questions: "Am I happy? Is what I have captured worth everything I have given up so far?" In fact, it may be too late to ask these questions, and in the end, if one has to answer 'no,' those who rushed toward the goals have, in fact, failed. Thus, we need to continue asking ourselves, "What am I living for?" and "What is at the root of my desire as I lead my life?"

The power of questioning helps us to examine our desires. This power of introspection makes us look back at blind passion and control speeding headlong in one direction. It also leads us to contemplate the true value of life. Through this contemplation, we take care of ourselves so that we can own our life. Josin's dream is the Silla version of the story about the journey of self-reflection.

Even though I Dreamed of Happiness, I Fell into Unhappiness

Josin was a monk in the Buddhist temple Segyu, located in Nalligun, Myeongju, in Silla. A governor's daughter often visited the temple to pray to Buddha. Josin was attracted to her and prayed that his love for her would be realized, which was wrong for him to do as a monk. Meanwhile, he heard the news that the governor's daughter would be married. Josin blamed the Buddhist Goddess of Mercy for not having listened to his wish and he fell asleep in tears. In his dream, Josin met with the daughter of the governor. She confessed that it was Josin who she truly loved. They then escaped and began a life together. They were happy for a while. However, as they had five children while living together, they could not escape from poverty. Ultimately, the first child died from hunger, and a daughter died after going out begging and being attacked by a dog. Josin and his wife had left for happiness but found themselves in misery. The couple cried over and over. The wife then made a decision to separate. Deep down Josin felt pleased and relieved. He also had been in agony. When they were about to leave to go their own ways, Josin woke up and realized that everything was a dream. In that one

Hongryeonam (left) and Haesu Gwaneumsang (The statue of the Buddhist Goddess of Mercy) (right)
The left side is a hermitage, Hongryeonam, of the Naksan temple, which appeared in *'Josin's dream'* in *Samgukyusa*. The right side is the statue of Buddhist Goddess of Mercy, looking out over the sea.

Josin's Dream

night, his hair and beard had turned white. Because he had lived his whole life in one day, his body had aged. His mental state was foggy and his will had disappeared. He felt embarrassed that he had dreamed of secular life and had made a greedy wish as a monk. He repented again and again.

Even though he had wished for happiness, the only things left for Josin are a miserable life and debilitated body. He had a passion for being happy but inscribed in his body was the shadow of unhappiness and the trace of cruel time and tide. Josin went to where he had buried his child in his dream and dug into the ground. There he found a stone statue of the Future Buddha (Sanskrit: Maitreya). The statue of the Future Buddha symbolizes that even a trace of misery can be a medium of enlightenment. Josin washed the statue of Buddha and placed it in the neighboring temple. He then came to the capital, built the temple Jeongto with all of his assets, and turned down an official position. From that point on, he performed good deeds. No one knew where he ended his life.

Lee Gwang-su wrote a novel *Dream* (1947) based on Josin's dream in *Samgukyusa*.

Examine Passion and Desire

People commonly say that passion is the asset of youth, and a life spent focusing on a dream is beautiful. However, Josin's story presents

A Korean Movie, *Dream* (Directed by Bae Chang-ho, 1991). The movie was based on the original script of *Josin's dream*. The actor An Seong-gi, and the actress Hwang Shin-hye, played protagonists.

a different perspective. Passion itself is not beautiful, and sometimes it drives life's direction blindly and harshly. A dream can apparently be beautiful, but it also accompanies destructive aspects; it makes people blind or deaf to precious things while they are only focusing on their dream. Passion and desire are not beautiful by themselves; they need to be objects of self-reflection. In the long journey of life, we need to repeatedly ask the question: "Am I living well now? Do I exist in the right way?"

Josin's dream tells us that a life spent chasing desire is empty. We can own our life by asking what exists at the end point of life and what kind of value the things we pursue eventually have.

Even though I dreamed of happiness, I fell into unhappiness.

Happiness and unhappiness depends on oneself in the end. The governor's daughter appearing in Josin's dream was an illusion, like bubbles created by Josin's desire. On the one hand, it can be analyzed

Josin's Dream

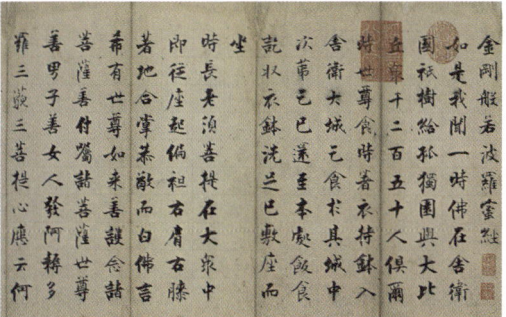

Geumganggyeong (Diamond Sutra).
The sutra that provided philosophical background of the Buddhist concept of *gong* (emptiness).

as the incarnate of the Buddhist Goddess of Mercy to whom Josin offered an empty prayer. She appeared in his dream to make him realize that his desire is in vain and guided him to experience the end of life while pursuing desire. Nonetheless, Josin's prayer was not useless. The response from the Buddhist Goddess of Mercy was accomplished not by making his wish come true but by leading Josin to realize the emptiness. The lady in his dream was, so to speak, knowledge of Zen.

In summary, the story of Josin's dream delivers the following message: Self-reflect and self-reflect again. Reflect on yourself self-reflecting. Then you can stay in the present. Only those who reflect on the self until they reach the moment experiencing the full state of emptiness will own their true life.

"In general, every form is all empty. If you recognize all the forms as no forms, you will see Buddha."

From *Geumganggyeong (Diamond Sutra) Saguge*

Kim Hyeon Gam Ho:
The Love between Kim Hyeon and a Lady Tiger

During the Silla period, it was customary for men and women in the capital to pray for good fortune by circling around the tower of the temple called Heungryun between February 8th and 15th in the lunar calendar. One night, during King Wonseong's regime in Silla, a fellow named Kim Hyeon circled the tower alone without stopping. Suddenly, a lady began to follow him, praying. They became attracted to one other and began staring at each other. When they had finished circling the tower, they went to a place where they could avoid other people and share their love. When the lady tried to leave, Kim Hyeon offered to accompany her. However, the woman refused his offer and insisted on going alone. Kim Hyeon followed her in spite of her refusal.

When the lady reached the foot of a mountain in the west, she entered a thatched house. There was an old woman inside and she asked, "Who is this man with you?" The lady told the truth about what had happened. Then the old woman said, "This may seem like a good thing for you, but it might have been better if it had never happened at all. However, what can we do? The things that happened, happened. Please hide him well. I am afraid of what would happen if your brothers were to become aware of it."

The lady hid him in a secret place.

A little later, three tigers appeared growling. They spoke with human voices. "We smell something in the house. It would be great for us to have something to eat."

The old woman and the lady scolded them, "Your noses must be off. Are you crazy?"

Then they heard a voice saying, "You enjoy killing too much. To punish you, one of you will die."

The three tigers who had been growling before became worried when they heard this.

Then the lady said, "If the three of you run away and punish yourselves, I will take the punishment instead of you."

The three tigers felt relieved. They lowered their heads and tails and ran away.

The lady came to Kim Hyeon and said, "I was so embarrassed that you would learn about the secret of my family from the beginning. Now, however, I don't have anything to hide, and so I will tell you the truth. Even though you and I belong to different species, we shared the pleasure of one night, which was similar to the love of a couple. Since the Heaven hates my brothers' wickedness, I would like to take responsibility for this misfortune in my family. However, I would rather die at your hands than at the hands of some stranger's so that I can pay back all the love and grace you have given to me. So please listen carefully to what I say. I will raise a fuss at the market by pretending that I will hurt people. Then the public will feel threatened and their peace will be disturbed, and they will be unable to control me. When this happens, the king will recruit people to catch me by promising a high official rank in return. Please do not be afraid of me. Chase me into the woods north from the castle. I will wait for you there."

Kim Hyeon said, "It is a natural law that humans court only humans. Even though we belong to different species, we courted. This was not an appropriate thing to do. However, we have already made love to each other without any problem, and we are very lucky. Given this, how can I acquire an official position and salary by trading them for my spouse's death?"

Then the woman said, "Please do not say that. It is Heaven's order that I die young. My wish is to expiate my brothers' sin through death, and I cannot wish it more if I could die at your hands. If you can gain an official position and perform a meritorious deed for the country, it will be a praiseworthy thing. In addition, it will be a fortune for my family to save my three brothers' lives. The public in this country will no longer be hurt by tigers, and they will enjoy peace. With my death, there are five advantages. How can I go against this? If you can build a Buddhist temple after I die and recite the Buddhist chants for me to amass good deeds, I will be overwhelmed by your grace."

After her speech, the two of them cried and said goodbye to each other. The next day, a violent tiger entered into the castle and went around hurting people. No one could handle the tiger. At this news, King Wonseong ordered, "I will give a reward to the person who catches the tiger."

Kim Hyeon reached the palace and told the king, "I will be able to complete that task."

Then the king encouraged him by first endowing him with a position. Kim Hyeon took a sword in his hands and followed the tiger to the woods. Then the tiger changed into the lady and said with a smile, "Please do not forget what we shared last night. Tell the people who were hurt today to dab soybean sauce of temple Heungryun on their scars and to listen to the trumpet sound of the temple. Then they will recover completely."

Finishing her speech, the lady stabbed herself in the neck with Kim Hyeon's sword and then she changed into a tiger. Kim Hyeon carried the tiger out of the woods saying, "I caught this tiger easily."

He kept the secret of the relationship between him and the woman. He informed the people of what she had told him, and the people who had been hurt by the tiger were cured. Nowadays (it was the Goryeo period during which *Samgukyusa* was being written), the same kind of folk remedy is used when people are bitten by a tiger.

After Kim Hyeon obtained the official position, he built a Buddhist temple near the bank of the Seocheon River and named the temple Howon, meaning 'a tiger's wish.' Then he arranged for the chant *Beommanggyeong* to always be recited so that the tiger could go to a good place after death. Thus, he tried to pay back the tiger's grace in which she had saved others by killing herself.

Time passed by and when Kim Hyeon became old, he wrote an autobiography about the mysterious thing he had experienced in the past. Then the story was made public. The title of the story is

"A Story of the Tiger Forest" and it is still being passed down in the present day. (It was during the Goryeo period that *Samgukyusa* was written.)

Origin   Ilyeon, 'Kim Hyeon Gam Ho,' 〈*Gamtong*〉, *Samgukyusa*

Commentaries

Love of a Lady Tiger that is more Humanistic than that of Humans

Contemplation on the Boundary between Humans and Non-Humans

As science and technology develop, the boundary between humans and machines is obscured. Consider a Go match between the South Korean professional Go player Lee Se-dol, and artificial intelligence machine, AlphaGo, held in Korea in 2016. Go (*baduk* in Korean) is representative of a game that requires the most creative human strategies. AlphaGo won all but one in a five-game match, demonstrating how machines are gradually replacing humans, excelling, and even overwhelming them. In medicine, machines are already becoming parts of the human body; the development of technology and engineering allows machinery, such as prosthetic arms, artificial hearts, artificial kidneys, etc., inside human bodies. In the daily lives of humans, all things are becoming connected with the

Movie, *The Matrix* (1999)   Movie, *Blade Runner* (1982)

internet through smartphones and IoT (Internet of Things). However, humans and machines are not forming a symbiotic relationship.

The relationship between a human and a machine comprises various networks of opposition, assistance, and collaboration. As the machines intervene in human life and permeate the human body and time, humans encounter situations in which they must redefine their identity. As machines become humanized, the boundary between human vs. non-human is blurred. The science fiction classic *Blade Runner* (1982) directed by Ridley Scott has already proposed exploring this sort of question. Filmographic imagination introspecting the question of 'What is a human?' through cyborgs more humanistic than humans has continued in movies such as *Ghost in the Shell*,[1] *Gattaca*,[2] and *The Matrix*[3] all the while generating follow-up questions.

As the boundary between humans and machines becomes

---

1   Directed by Oshima Mamoru in 1995, Remaked by Rupert Sanders in 2017
2   Directed by Andrew Niccole, 1997
3   Directed by Lana Wachowski and Lily Wachowski, 1999

obscured, questions about humanity are intensified. Interestingly, this phenomenon is not paradoxical but natural; it is traditional as opposed to belonging to a machine civilization. The relevant example can be found in the story of *Kim Hyeon Gam Ho* in *Samgukyusa*.

A Lesson through the Lady Tiger's Love

This story deals with a romance between Kim Hyeon and a lady tiger. It is a romantic narrative composed of philosophical reflections on the boundary between humans and non-humans. The lady tiger that Kim Hyeon loved belongs to a cat species that is represented with animalistic brutality, wildness, and violence. However, her mind, spirit, language, facial expressions, and attitudes demonstrate the most sublime humanistic values; this triggers a sense of confusion. What is a human? How different is 'being a human' than 'being humanistic?' If there is an animal that is more humanistic, how do we need to treat him or her?

Kim Hyeon fell in love with the lady tiger while circling the pagoda[4] in the Heungryun temple. The two of them fell in love with each other instantly the moment that they met due to intuitive insight and recognition of each other's identity, not calculation of the other party's condition or family background. Emotions were the

---

4 It is a Buddhist tradition to circle a pagoda all night on the Buddha's birthday while commemorating the Buddha's merit and virtuosity and praying for individual wishes. The Buddhist ritual evolved into a folk play.

only medium. The love between the two was life changing because they had to accept love between a human and a tiger. This story implies that emotion is not the medium of momentary pleasure and interaction but is one of life's deciding factors.[5] When Kim Hyeon arrived at the lady tiger's house, he felt her family members were violent tigers targeting his life. For the tiger brothers, the younger sister's lover was not a family member but prey. They snarled and wanted Kim Hyeon's life. This is because the tiger brothers were brutal animals, but also because Kim Hyeon symbolized the family's desire to feed off of him. In addition, it is a satire of the Silla society, which despised people of lower status as savages.[6]

Circling the Pagoda © Yonhap News

Kim Hyeon was to die as the tiger brothers' prey, and this tormented the lady tiger. If she ran away, her brothers would follow them and make a mess, and then the country would be in chaos. Even if Kim Hyeon was lucky enough to survive and her brothers were caught, her mother would lose her sons and, like the lady tiger, would fall into despair. In contrast, if the lady tiger left her brothers to eat Kim Hyeon, she would experience a horrible loss. The lady

---

5   That is also why Koreans have traditionally discussed emotional regulation, control, and management.

6   Silla was the society with a status system called *golpumje*.

tiger was faced with a dilemma. What should she do?

The lady tiger presented a brilliant idea in which no one would get hurt. She tried her best to calm down her brothers, who were excited by the smell of meat, and to keep her love by saving Kim Hyeon. She also needed a way to save people who were distressed by tiger attacks and soothe her mother by saving her three sons from crisis. She thought it was her time to die and that this was her destiny to follow. The lady tiger chose her path to sacrifice herself.

The lady tiger told Kim Hyeon that she would make a big fuss by pretending to hurt people. This would lead the king to look for someone to solve the problem and to offer a high official position in exchange. She told him to catch her and offer her to the king when that happened. If he followed her instructions, she added, Kim Hyeon would have a high official position, the lives of her three brothers would be saved, and people would not be hurt. She asked him to build a temple for her and to preach Buddhist sutras so that she could accumulate good karma. According to her, this is the way for everyone to achieve happiness.

Kim Hyeon refused her favor immediately. He said "It went against moral laws to become involved with a tiger as a human. Because I truly loved you, I have no regrets. On the contrary, I am so lucky to have felt true love. However, it is not the right thing to do to gain an official position and allowance in exchange for a spouse's life." Since Kim Hyeon admitted that she was his life partner, the lady tiger felt as though she had heard a confession of his love. In the end, the lady tiger chose to sacrifice herself by killing herself in front of

Kim Hyeon. Choking back his tears, Kim Hyeon presented her dead body, which had turned into a tiger, to the king. Then he offered a treatment method to the people. Since that time, people have learned how to treat and cure tiger bites. The lady tiger found a creative idea to benefit everyone through her self-sacrifice. The lady tiger's behavior was not that of an animal, so-called barbaric, inhumane, and brutal, but more humane and sacred than humans.

Now, let's look at Kim Hyeon's story. After the lady tiger died, how did Kim Hyeon, who was left alone, live? This story skips the details. Did he live happily ever after enjoying a luxurious life with a high position and allowance in return for her death? Although the story does not say, we may predict how he lived based upon his behavior at the end. Kim Hyeon built a temple in accordance with the lady tiger's wish and named it Howon,[7] which means 'tiger's wish.' The tiger's wish was to overcome the existential limit of animality. It was to follow the sacred and holy road to save parents, siblings, a lover or a husband, people, and the country.

The tiger's wish was to go beyond the limitations of species and tigerhood and to become the most sacred being. In order to represent her wish and commemorate it, Kim Hyeon built a temple and preached a Buddhist sutra named *Beommanggyeong*.[8] He wanted to repay her sacrifice by praying for her rebirth in paradise. Kim Hyeon kept his story a secret until he reached old age. If he had told anyone

---

7   Temple Howon was built in Silla period, and the temple was located in Gyeongju, Gyeongsangbukdo Province. Nowadays, there are only the remains of the site where two pagodas were, and the cornerstones are scattered about in the area where Howon temple presumably was.

8   *Beommanggyeong* is a Mahayana sutra specifying the Buddhist commandments.

The Tripitaka Koreana in the Haein temple
© Cultural Heritage Administration

the facts at the time, he could have been a target of dishonor and been accused of being a liar or a prodigal who had sex with a tiger. Obviously their noble love would have been insulted. Kim Hyeon kept the secret to himself and lived his life in silence. As he approached death, he wrote his story and shared it with people. Because the story was treasured in his heart for a long time, it was received by people as a heart-breaking personal history and honorable memory rather than as an object of scorn or a mysterious rumor. His sincere efforts to build a temple and to pray for the tiger lady's spirit for the rest of his life touched people's hearts. The noble will of the secret keeper was transmitted in full.

Human's Way and Humane Way of Life

The lady tiger who had been more humanistic than humans lead us to introspect over the boundary between a human and a non-human. Then it presents us with a fundamental question, 'What is it to be humanistic?' Kim Hyeon who fell in love with a tiger showed the most beautiful and sacred humane conduct. Through his behavior, he brought us to reflect over the sublimity and greatness of love. Momentary love dominated and changed life entirely for the two.

Based upon the Buddhist philosophy, the intense narrative of love was transformed from a sensuous romance to a narrative of self-reflection. The remark made by the lady tiger's mother when Kim Hyeon first visited her house implies a profound message of the Buddhist philosophy.

"This may seem like a good thing for you, but it might have been better if it had never happened at all."

The remark shows an epistemological thought that even the best effort of a human is mere creation of karma. The act considered the most beautiful thing today may turn out to be an ugly one tomorrow. My happiness may be someone else's misery. Therefore, humans should always be penitent and introspective for themselves and others, while maintaining humble attitudes for the sake of society and history. Kim Hyeon survived, kept a life-long secret, and prayed for the lady tiger. His life itself was the journey of penitence. The lady tiger's mother, who had various experiences, seems to represent the voice of a sage who knew everything but kept watching, like the Oracle in the movie *The Matrix*. Although there was no technical advancement in mechanical engineering in the Silla period by comparison with today, there was introspective thinking over the relationship between humans and nonhumans and their symbiosis. The lady tiger was more humanistic than humans and sacrificed herself. Kim Hyeon kept his heart-breaking secret with great dignity and beautifully sublimated his personal wound. Through the lady tiger and Kim Hyeon's conduct, this story presents a philosophical question of what it means to be humanistic to a reader, who lives in a much later time.

Yi Saeng Gyu Jang Jeon:
The Story of Yi Saeng Peering Over the Wall

There lived a student whose last name was Yi near the bridge called Naktagyo in Songdo (nowadays, Gaeseong). He was eighteen years old with polite manners, natural talents, and intelligence. He attended Gukhak (a state university in those days), and he recited poems as he walked. Around the same time, there was a family with the last name Choe in a village called Seonjukri, who had high social status and wealth. Their sixteen old daughter was not only beautiful and attractive, but she also excelled in embroidery and in poetry and rhymes. People described them as follows:

For refinement and taste in the arts, Yi's son is the best.
For elegance and ladylike grace, Choe's daughter is the first.
Her style and figure are the finest;
Simply watching her makes us full.

Yi Saeng Gyu Jang Jeon: The Story of Yi Saeng Peering Over the Wall

Yi Saeng went to school in the early morning with his book under his arm. He always passed the house of Choe Rang (meaning Lady Choe). Dozens of willow trees were lined up surrounding the outside of the northern wall of the house. Whenever the wind blew, the leaves rustled in the breeze. Yi Saeng used to stop and rest under a tree.

One day, on his way to school, Yi Saeng happened to peer over the wall briefly. There were gorgeous flowers all in bloom, while bees and birds were chattering, flying all over. Through luxuriant flowering bushes, he saw a pavilion located on the side. The pavilion was half covered by a jade blind and a silk curtain screen. Inside, a gorgeous lady was doing embroidery. She stopped her hands and recited a poem, resting her cheeks on her hands.

While leaning alone against a silk window pane and embroidering
I hear an oriole sing in a glorious forest of flowers.
Secretly resenting the spring breeze,
I rest the needle and fall into thought.

The young student out there on his way! To which family does he belong?
His blue coat and wide belt glimmer through the willow.
If I could turn into a sparrow and fly along the pavilion,
I would pass through the bead curtains and fly over the wall.

Upon hearing her poem, Yi Saeng could not help showing off his talents. However, the gate to the house was lofty and magnificent. The women's residence was quite deep in the yard and far away. He felt sorry that he had to leave for school. On his way back, he threw a white paper with a piece of roofing tile inside the wall. On the paper, he had written three stanzas. The poem went like this:

Among the twelve mountain peaks of Musan covered in layers of streaming fog
A red and blue light shimmers in a peak exposed halfway.
I fear the longing in my heart will turn into King Yang's lonely dream[1]
And my love will meet me at Yangdae[2] *as clouds and rain.*

Like Samasangyeo seducing Takmungun,[3]
My anxious love fills my heart to bursting!
Adorned in red and in full bloom, the peach and plum blossoms on the wall
Spread their petals as they drift in the wind.

---

1 An old story in the Cho period of China. King Hwe, who was the father of King Yang, held a party in Godanggwan and fell asleep. In his dream, he fell in love with a fairy of Musan. When the time came to separate, the woman said she would become clouds in the morning and rain in the evening while missing him, and she disappeared. When King Hwe woke up, there were beautiful clouds on the peak of the mountain just as the woman had told him. King Yang's lonely dream refers to the dream about falling in love with a beautiful fairy woman.

2 Yangdae literally refers to "the sunny peak," but means secret love in this context.

3 It refers to the episode in which Takmungun fell in love with Samasangyeo upon hearing him playing the *geomungo* (a musical instrument).

Will fate be kind or cruel?
In my empty heart a day feels like a year.
Four line stanzas declare our love
But will I ever meet my hermit in Namgyo?[4]

Choe Rang heard something drop, and she asked her servant Hyangah to go and fetch it. Hyangah brought the note hanging from a piece of roofing tile. Choe Rang unfolded the note and found it was the poem sent by Yi Saeng. Choe Rang read the poem again and again. She was thrilled and pleased. She also made a note and sent it to Yi Saeng. It said, "Please do not be suspicious. I would like to meet around sunset."

Yi Saeng visited her house following the instructions in her letter. Suddenly, he saw a branch with peach flowers swaying over the wall and casting a shadow. Upon coming closer, Yi Saeng saw a bamboo basket hanging down from a swinging rope made of flannel. Yi Saeng grabbed the rope and climbed up and over the wall. At just that moment, the moon crested the hill, and the lovely shadows of flowers spreading fragrance all around were reflected on the ground. Yi Saeng felt as if he had entered the world of hermits, and he enjoyed a secret thrill. At the same time, however, he felt

---

4 Namgyo is the name of a Chinese province. It is said that during the Tang Dynasty, Bae Hang met Wun Young there. He was attracted to Wun Young, but he had to make hermit's medicine for 100 days before he could marry her. After that, they became hermits and left together.

nervous as he remembered that this meeting was surreptitious.

As Yi Saeng looked all around, he found Choe Rang shyly smiling at him. She was already sitting at the corner of the flowering woods with Hyangah, and they were pinning flowers into each other's hair. Choe Rang had written a two-line poem first, and she sang it like a song.

Oh, peach flowers, plum flowers! Those charming blossoms.
Over pillows embroidered with love birds a clear moon rises.

Yi Saeng added two more lines.

Some day if word of spring slips out
A cruel rainstorm will blow it out.

Upon hearing this song, Choe Rang turned red and said, "From the beginning, I have wanted to be your wife and to live happily ever after with you. Why would you make such a weak remark? I am a woman, but I feel calm. Why do you with the spirit of a strong man say such a thing? Even if I am criticized by my parents, I will take responsibility."

Then she said to Hyangah, "Hyangah! Please go to the room and bring us some drinks and fruit."

Hyangah left to retrieve the order. Everything was so quiet and calm without any human sound. Yi Saeng asked Choe Rang, "Where are we?"

Choe Rang replied, "This is a small pavilion located in the

northern garden. My parents love me so much that they built this pavilion near a pond called Buyongji. When spring comes, famous flowers bloom and I spend much time here with my maid. Since my parents are far, far away from here, they cannot hear us even if we laugh loudly or chat."

Choe Rang poured a small drink and asked Yi Saeng to drink it as she improvised a poem.

Looking down at Buyongji while leaning over a curved rail
I hear through the flowers on the pond people whispering of love.
In the fine spring scene, a fragrant fog gently spreads like a veil,
And they write new words for the love song they sing.
On a floor cushion in the shadows of flowers, the moon throws its beams;
As the lovers pull aside a long branch a shower of rain flowers scatters,
As my silk summer jacket brushes a branch of sweetbriers
A surprised parrot hiding in the flowers flaps away.

Yi Saeng quickly replied with his poem.

Flowers are in full bloom in the hermit's world I intrude upon.
How could I ever tell you everything in my heart?
I stuck a golden hairpin in my daintily braided hair
And with a skein of green ramie cloth I made a willowy spring doublet.

The spring wind blew and snapped the flowers blooming side by side,
So please, Rainy Wind, do not shake the stems.
Oh, the fluttering shadow of a fairy's sleeve!
A fairy dances in the shadow of a cinnamon tree grove.
Before a good deed is done, worries breed in my mind.
So don't write a new song to teach the bird of love.

When Yi Saeng finished, Choe Rang said, "It is an uncommon destiny that we meet today. Please follow me and make our love come true."

Upon finishing her remark, she entered a window on the northern side and Yi Saeng followed her. There was a ladder going up to the pavilion in the room. As they went up the ladder, an attic appeared. Inside there was a desk and stationery arranged neatly and cleanly. On one side of the walls, two pictures were hanging; one was a picture of mountains layered in fog and the other was a picture of a secluded bamboo grove and a withered tree. Both of them were masterpieces. There were poems on the top of the pictures, whose writer is unknown.

The poem in the first picture was as follows:

Who saved energy in the tip of his brush
Whose brush had the strength left in its tip
To draw a mountain range of a thousand ridges in the middle of a river?
Oh, Mountain Bangho[5] of thirty thousand gil![6] Grand and magnificent!
A peak rises above the far-off clouds,
The mountain range stretches hundreds of li.[7]
Like blue conch shells, the surrounding peaks spike and soar.

---

5 Mountain Bangho is a mountain where a hermit lives.
6 *Gil* is a unit measuring length. One *gil* corresponds to 10 or 8 *ja* (one *ja* is a Korean foot and is equal to 30.3cm).
7 *Li* is a unit measuring distance. One *li* corresponds to 0.393km.

Blue waves reach the far-away sky.
Looking at the sunset suddenly makes me homesick.
Watching the picture makes me lonely.
The boat on Sang River seems to be caught in a rainstorm.

The poem in the second picture was as follows:

In the lonely sound of wind passing through the thick bamboo groves
A lofty withered tree has long harbored lasting love.
Its winding roots are covered with moss,
Its old trunk has endured wind and thunder.
Traces of harmony linger inside of the tree.
But who can share its mysterious wisdom?
Alas, great painters like Wi Eon and Yeo Ga have passed away.
How many will recognize the secrets of nature the tree releases.
Sitting by a clear window and staring outside without a word,
I give myself to the mystery of nature's brush stroke.

On another side of the walls, there were four poems reciting about four seasons. The writer of them was also unknown. The style of calligraphy was similar to Cho Maeng-bu's,[8] and it was neat and beautiful. The first poem was as follows:

---

8 Cho Maeng-bu is a Chinese calligrapher in the Yuan Dynasty in China. In Chinese, his name is pronounced as 'Zhao Mengfu.'

The screen curtain printed with lotus flowers feels so soft and its fragrance floats so gently.
Outside the window red blossoms of apricot softly drizzle like rain.
As the bell of dawn awakens me, a dream lingers in my head.
From the bank full of magnolia blossoms, I hear the song of a dusky thrush.

As a baby swallow grows, night deepens in the boudoir.
Languor comes and I stop embroidering without a word.
A pair of swallowtail butterflies flying below the flowers
Flies along the falling flowers,
The flower shadows are flapping over the garden.
As a spring cold gently seeps into my green skirt
My heart aches at the lonely spring wind.
Who will understand my lonesome heart?
Now, a pair of lovebirds dances among flower blossoms!

The world is bright with full spring light
Deep pinks and yellow greens reflect in the silk screen.
With flowers and foliage filling the garden, spring fills me with sorrow.
Slightly rolling up the screen curtain, I stare at the falling flowers.

The second poem was as follows:

Baby swallows fly into budding ears of wheat.

All over the south garden pomegranate flowers are in full bloom.
I hear a lady weaving near the window tinted with green.
Is she making a red skirt by cutting up purple clouds?

It is the season when green plums ripen.
Raindrops fall softly.
An oriole twitters in the shadow of a pagoda tree
And a swallow flies into the screen curtain.
So the scene of another year passes away.
As white cedar flowers wither, new bamboo shoots appear.

The green apricot in my hand, should I throw it to the baby oriole?
The wind passes through the southern balustrade and the sun's shadow is ready to set.
With the lotus leaves' fragrance gone, the pond is left full of only water.
A cormorant is bathing in the blue waves of a deep spot.

On the bamboo mat of a wisteria bower, a pattern of waves shimmers.
On the panels of the folding screen, cotton clouds billow on the Sosang River.
Awake from my afternoon slumber I feel hazy and languid still.
Between the half open window, the sun goes down little by little.

The third poem was as follows:

Yi Saeng Gyu Jang Jeon: The Story of Yi Saeng Peering Over the Wall

The fall wind blows and cold dew falls in drops.
Oh, the beautiful light of the fall moon. The water of fall is so blue.
Wild geese return home crying sadly.
I listen to it again, the sound of paulownia leaves falling into a well.

Under the day bed, a batch of bugs clatter.
On the day bed, a beautiful woman sheds tears like jade.
My dear love, who is in the battlefield tens of thousands of miles away,
Please look at the moon light that falls tonight on Okmungwan.[9]

As I cut cloth for new clothes, the scissors feel cold.
Dear maid, please bring me an iron, I whispered low;
I didn't realize the iron was cold.
With a slender string bow I only scratch my hair.

In a small pond, lotus flowers wither and plantain leaves turn yellow.
On the roof tiles embossed with love birds, the first frost forms.
Old worries and new sorrows find me out.
The chirping of crickets reaches deep into this hidden room.

The fourth poem was as follows:

---

9 Okmungwan is a gate near Donhwang-hyeon in Ancient China. It was situated in an area near the national border, so there were frequent wars with other countries.

A branch of plum flowers throws its shadow on the window.
How bright the moonlight is on the servant quarters to the windy west.
After tending the fire in the brazier with tongs,
I turn around and call a young maid to change the tea pot.
Leaves in the forest fall from a sudden night frost.
Snowflakes fly in the swirling wind and blow into the long corridor.
Tonight is an endless night of dreaming of my love.
It seems I stand on an ancient glacier battlefield.

The full red light on the window feels warm like spring
And brings sleep to my care-laden eyes.
The plum tree branch in the vase sends out a half-opened bud.
Feeling shy, I quietly embroider turtle doves.[10]

A frosty wind passes through the northern forest.
A crow cries over a cold moon and my heart aches.
While sewing in front of an oil lamp I weep for my love.
The tear drops soak the thread and hang like pearls on the needle.

There was a small room on one side with a beautiful curtain screen, a comforter, mattress, and pillows neatly arranged. On the other side of the screen, incense of musk was burning and its fragrance surrounded the room. The room was as bright as day from the light

---

10 In the original text, a word referring to mandarin ducks has been used instead.

of a lamp fragrant with oil. Yi Saeng made love with Choe Rang and they had a great time together.

One day, after staying together several days, Yi Saeng said to Choe Rang, "According to an old sage's advice, we should let our parents know where we are going when we leave. I haven't greeted my parents for the last three days. My parents must be waiting for me in town. This is contrary to my filial piety as a child."

Although Choe Rang was sad, she allowed him to leave and let him jump over the wall. From that time on, he didn't miss a single day without visiting her in the evening.

One evening, Yi Saeng's father asked, "You used to leave in the morning and come back around sunset to learn the teachings of sages. However, these days, you leave home around sunset and come back at dawn. What is wrong with you? It is obvious that you are going over the wall and misbehaving. When others learn about this, they will criticize me and your mother as having misguided a child. It seems that that woman's family is noble with high status. Since your imprudent behavior dishonors our family and disturbs us, this is no small thing. Go to Youngnam Province and manage our farm and watch over the servants. Do not even think about coming back."

The next day, Yi Saeng was sent to Ulju in Youngnam Province. Choe Rang waited for Yi Saeng every evening at the garden with flower blossoms. However, he didn't come for several months. She worried that Yi Saeng might have happened to become sick, so she secretly sent Hyangah to question Yi Saeng's neighbors. His neighbors said, "Mr. Yi committed a sin against his father and was sent to Youngnam Province several months ago."

At this news, Choe Rang fell sick and lay in her bed. She was unable to get up and couldn't eat even thin rice gruel. She was unable to speak well. Her skin looked pale and tired. Her parents thought that it was not normal, and they asked her for a reason. Yet, she didn't say anything. One day, her parents opened a box in their daughter's room. In the box, there were poems she had exchanged with Yi Saeng. Finally, her parents figured out what the situation was and exclaimed in surprise, "Oh, we almost lost our daughter."

They asked their daughter, "Who is Yi Saeng?"

At that moment, Choe Rang could no longer hide things from her parents. She spoke to her parents in her thin weak voice, "How can I hide things from you in spite of all your grace raising me? I have spent time thinking to myself and have realized that among the various human relationships, it is extremely valuable for a man and a woman to feel love. Thus, the old books say that the timing of marriage should not be delayed and that decency requires a woman to be chaste.

My weakness, however, was like a willow and I didn't think carefully about how my body would be hurt. I lost my virginity and have been laughed at by neighbors. Because I depended on a man, like moss depending on a tree, my sin has seriously damaged the name of my family. With all of this, my heart is full of blame for that hateful man ever since I once made love with him. I have endured worry, and I live helplessly with my weak body. However, my love for him grows deeper every day and my illness worsens. It has reached a point where I feel as though I might die. Now I will become a poor ghost. If you accept my wish to be together with him, then I will be able to save my life. However, if you ask me to quit my love for him, there is only one way for me to die. I would rather meet Yi Saeng again in the world of death than marry someone else."

Choe Rang's parents understood their daughter's mind. Thus, they did not ask about her illness and calmed her down by talking to her and soothing her. They followed formal courtesy and proposed to Yi Saeng by sending a matchmaker.

Yi Saeng's father asked about Choe's family and said, "My son is young and immature, but good at scholarly work and equipped with proper manners and attitudes. He will become famous later on after he passes the exam for government officials. Thus, we are in no hurry to find him a spouse."

The matchmaker reported the words as heard. Then, Choe's family sent the matchmaker again and asked, "My friends all praised your son for his excellent talents. Even though his name is unknown as of yet, why will he stay a hidden man? We wish to have a wedding ceremony by matching these two beautiful people, who are destined to be a couple."

The matchmaker came to Yi Saeng's father and delivered what had been heard. Then Yi Saeng's father said,

"I also worked hard with all the sacred books when I was young. But I haven't succeeded until this old age. All the servants ran away and my relatives rarely helped me. As a result, my household is badly off and looks poor. Why would a powerful family like yours want to have a poor scholar as a son-in-law? It seems clear that rumormongers have praised my family too much and have tried to cause trouble for you."

The matchmaker went back and delivered the message as heard. Choe's father said, "We will prepare for wedding presents and clothes. We hope to pick a fortunate day and have a ceremony." The matchmaker delivered what was said upon returning to Yi Saeng's father. Under these circumstances, Yi Saeng's father changed his mind and sent a person to call on his son in order to ask his opinion. Yi Saeng couldn't hide his pleasure. He wrote a poem to express his mind.

> *Since the broken mirror has been put back together, our reunion has come true.*
> *Heaven's Ojakgyo*[11] *has aided this beautiful reunion.*
> *Now that Old Wolha*[12] *has tied together the threads of fate,*
> *Do not begrudge the cuckoo in the spring wind.*

At this news, Choe Rang became better little by little. She also wrote a poem and replied.

> *Miserable destiny has turned fortunate.*

---

[11] Ojakgyo is a bridge that appears in a myth. It was made by crows and magpies to help a loving couple, Gyeonwu and Jiknyeo, with their reunion once a year on July 7th.

[12] The Old Wolha is a matchmaker who connects couples.

The World of Fantasy

The promise I made is finally accomplished.
When will the day come to pull the little wagon together?
Dear girl, please let me sit so that I can arrange my hairpin.

Finally, they set a fortunate day, held a wedding ceremony, and continued to love each other. The couple lived together, and loved and respected each other by pleasantly treating each other as if they were guests. All other couples could not compete with their fidelity and loyalty. The next year Yi Saeng passed the exam for government officials and took office. His name became highly reputed.

In the year of Sinchuk, Chinese robbers, *honggeonjeok*, attacked the capital and the king escaped to Gyeongsang Province. The enemy burned houses, killed people, and slaughtered livestock and ate them. The couple and their relatives could not protect one another, and they ran away separately to the east or west. Yi Saeng took his family and hid in a secluded mountain. Then a robber chased them with a sword in hand. Although Yi Saeng managed to avoid him, Choe Rang was caught. When the robber tried to force himself on Choe Rang, she scolded him in a loud voice, "Oh, filthy bastard, please kill me and eat me. I would rather have my funeral inside of a wolf or a wild dog. How would it be possible for me to be a mate of a filthy pig like you?"

The furious enemy killed Choe Rang and cut away her flesh.

Yi Saeng, who had run away to a desolate field, managed to survive, and he went back to his old house to find his parents after hearing that the enemy had been defeated and had left. However, his parents' house had already been burned. He then went to the house in which he and his wife lived. Only the noise of mice and birds was left in the quarters where the servants had lived. Yi Saeng couldn't bear the sadness, and he shed tears in a small pavilion. Then he stopped crying and breathed only in deep sighs.

As night fell, he sat alone and thought about the old, pleasant days. Everything seemed to be a dream. As the night became deeper, the moonlight added its dim shine while reflecting the girder of the house. All of a sudden, the noise of foot steps could be heard from the hallway. The sound came closer and closer. When the sound stopped, Choe Rang was standing in front of him. Yi Saeng knew that she had died, but his love for her was so deep that he didn't reveal his suspicious mind to her. Yi Saeng asked Choe Rang, "Where did you go in order to survive?"

Choe Rang held his hands and wailed. She recovered her composure and opened her mouth.

"I was originally a woman from a good family. From the time I was young, I learned embroidery and knitting by following the guidance of my family. I also studied poetry and writing as well as manners. However, I only learned how to control domestic chores, not the things outside of my house. Ever since you peered over the wall with reddish apricot flowers, I have devoted my pearl of the blue sea to you. We smiled in front of flowers and had the relationship of a lifetime. When we had our reunion behind a curtain screen, it seemed that our love would last forever.

As I am telling you this, I cannot hold my miserable heart. I wanted to live to be a hundred years old with you. However, I didn't know this kind of mishap would happen, and I fell into a trench. Although I was not contaminated by the enemy like wild dogs, my body was torn in the mud. I could not endure that cruelty as a human. When I parted from you in the secluded mountain, I became a bird that lost its mate. My family fell into ruin and my parents passed away. I became a spirit who was hurt and tired and didn't have anyone to depend on. Since fidelity is precious and life is just nothing, I only thought that I was fortunate to escape the disgrace with my physical weakness. Who would pity my mind if it were split in pieces? I kept my mind as my guts were torn into pieces. My remains were thrown into the field, and my guts, on the street. While recounting all the pleasures I enjoyed, it seems that they existed for this sadness. Now spring wind blows into this deep mountain, and I have come back to this world again. Since my promise to you is firm and our destiny to love three times is so fragrant, I would like to have another relationship with you and keep our original vow. If you haven't forgotten it, I will keep this love forever. Would you allow me to do this?"

Yi Saeng was so pleased and touched at hearing this. He told her, "It is my true wish."

They intimately opened their minds to each other. As they talked about various things, he mentioned how many assets they had lost. Then Choe Rang said, "I didn't lose our things. I buried them in a mountain."

Yi Saeng asked, "Where are the remains of my parents and yours?"

Choe Rang answered, "I have kept them in a place."

They finished their warm conversation and went to bed. The pleasure was as usual. The next day, Choe Rang visited the place where she kept the parents' remains. In addition to their remains, there were some gold and silver ingots and several treasures. They collected both their parents' remains, sold the gold and treasures, and buried their parents together near the foot of Mt. Ogwan. Then they planted trees and held a memorial service with utmost manners.

After that, Yi Saeng did not seek an official position, but lived with Choe Rang. Meanwhile, the servants who had run away came back again. From that time on, Yi Saeng lost his interest in the human world. He didn't come out of his house even though there was important family business. He always exchanged poems with Choe Rang and spent a pleasant time with her in great harmony. Many years passed.

One evening, Choe Rang said to Yi Saeng, "I had a beautiful relationship with you three times. However, I cannot handle things in the world as I have wanted to. It is time to have a sad goodbye again even though the pleasure hasn't ended."

Finishing her words, Choe Rang wailed. Yi Saeng asked in surprise. "What do you mean?"

Choe Rang answered, "Destiny is inevitable. God permitted me to be reborn since our affinity was strong and I hadn't committed any sins. I could enjoy life for a moment with you. However, I can no longer stay in the human world and delude people who are alive."

Choe Rang asked her maid to bring a drink. Then she sang to the music called *Okruchungok* and asked Yi Saeng to drink. The song was as follows:

> *In the battlefield full of swords and spears,*
> *Cracked jade and fallen flowers strewed the land, and turtle doves lost their mates.*
> *Who will bury the skeletons littered everywhere?*
> *The wandering spirit stained with blood has nowhere to turn.*
>
> *The fairy of Musan who came down to Godang*
> *Grew wretched as the broken mirror split again.*
> *If we part like this, we will always stay far, far apart.*
> *No words will pass between heaven and humans.*

Whenever she sang the song, her tears fell in drops, and she couldn't finish the song. Yi Saeng said with deep sorrow.

"I would rather go to the heavens with you. How is it possible for me to stay alone and lead a meaningless life? During the last war, my family and servants scattered, and my parents' skeletons were spread all over the field. Without you, who would have held a memorial service for them? As the old people said, 'Respect your parents when they are alive and hold memorial rituals with complete decorums when they pass away.' You made great efforts in conducting all of them. You have an innate filial piety and generous mind. I am extremely moved and also ashamed. I hoped you would stay in the human world as long as you could and leave this world together with me as dirt after a hundred years."

Choe Rang replied, "You have more life remaining. However, my name is listed on the list of ghosts. I cannot stay here long. If I really miss the human world and hold a lingering attachment, it violates the heavenly laws. This is not only my fault, but also you will be affected. My skeleton must be scattered somewhere. If you want to bestow a favor on me, please take care of my bones so that they are not exposed to the wind and the sun."

Both of them stared at each other and shed tears.

"Goodbye, my dear love!"

After finishing her words, Choe Rang slowly went away. Then all trace of her was gone.

Yi Saeng collected her skeleton and buried the bones near her parents' graves. After her memorial service, Yi Saeng looked back on the past and became sick. He died in several months. People grieved over the news and everyone remembered their integrity and love.

<u>Origin</u> Kim Si-seup, 〈*Yi Saeng Gyu Jang Jeon*〉, *Geumosinhwa*

Commentaries

A House of a Ghost, Ontology of Extinction

A 15th Century Fantasy Story, Kim Si-seup's *Geumosinhwa*

This story, *Yi Saeng Gyu Jang Jeon*, is one of five stories included in *Geumosinhwa*,[1] a Sino-Korean short story created by a 15th century writer. The common factor in the stories in *Geumosinhwa* is fantasy. Those five stories present stories of exploration in which a ghost appears in real life and has a relationship with the main character, or the main character goes to the otherworld or the underwater palace of the Dragon King and experiences and associates with an unfamiliar world.

It is not unusual that the element of fantasy is involved in the

---

1   *Geumosinhwa* was written by Kim Si-seup (1435-1493).
    In addition to 〈*Yi Saeng Gyu Jang Jeon: The Story of Yi Saeng Peering Over the Wall*〉, there are 〈*Manboksajeopogi: Playing Jeopo at the Manbok temple*〉, 〈*Chwiyububyeokjeonggi: Playing Drunk in the Bubyeok Pavilion*〉, 〈*Namyeombujuji: the Story of Visiting the Otherworld (Yeombuju)*〉, and 〈*Yonggungbuyeonrok: the Story of Visiting a Party at the Underwater Palace of the Dragon King*〉.

narratives. However, it is extraordinary when the background is the Joseon period. This is because Confucian thoughts and Neo-Confucianism dominated the society, which prohibited imagination of the unrealistic fantasy world.² The intellectual of that time, Kim Si-seup, said "I will create fantastic stories, store them in a stone chamber, and wait 500 years." This remark results from this historical background.

A portrait of Kim Si-seup
© Cultural Heritage Administration

The Fantasy World of *Geumosinhwa*: Emotional Communion, Communication of Spirits, Acknowledgment of Presence

The main characters of the five short stories in *Geumosinhwa* are all young males who were outcasts from the real world or who did not reconcile with reality. They met and communed only with fantastic beings or a person who recognized them in a different world such as the otherworld or the palace of the Dragon King and shared with them sincere communication. In addition, they

---

2   Thoughts and study following Confucian teachings came to be the governing ideology of Joseon. Confucius mentioned *Goeryeoknansin* in the Analects of Confucius, which means he would not talk about prodigious things, violent things, confusing things, and mysterious things; thus, it was not considered appropriate for Joseon scholars (the literati and intellectuals) to talk about mysterious beings, the world of death, and fantastic space.

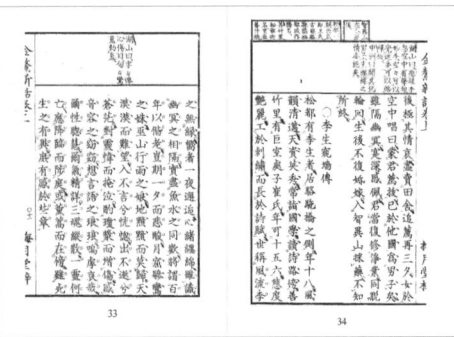

The printed version (1884) of *Geumosinhwa* is written in Chinese characters. © National Library of Korea

had intellectual discussions, formed intimate (sexual) relations, and received acknowledgment of their presences.

The main character Yi Saeng in *Yi Saeng Gyu Jang Jeon* chanced to peer over a wall, exchanged poems with Lady Choe, and fell in love with her. Even though they married against their parents' will, their happiness was momentary. A war soon broke out, and so they became separated; Lady Choe was murdered while fighting against a robber who tried to rape her. When the war ended and Yi Saeng came back home, Lady Choe appeared in front of him and they again resumed their love. Yi Saeng knew that his wife was a ghost, but pretended not to know it. As soon as he admitted that she was a ghost, he knew that they could not keep their love anymore. Love with a ghost was taboo.

Now, let us examine the other four stories included in *Geumosinhwa*.

The protagonist Yangsaeng in *Manboksajeopogi* (Playing *Jeopo* at the

Manbok Temple) requested a *Jeopo* game in a bet with Buddha, thought he won, and told Buddha his wish; Buddha could not throw *Jeopo*, so Yang Saeng could not help but win from the beginning. After asking to meet a beautiful woman, he hid behind Buddha. Then a beautiful woman came, bowed to Buddha, and made a wish for a good partner. This woman was actually a ghost who had committed suicide to keep her chastity when Japanese raiders had attacked. Yang Saeng roughly assumed she was a ghost but continued to love her anyway. This was because she became his soul mate after exchanging poetry with him.

In *Chwiyububyeokjeonggi* (Playing Drunk in the Bubyeok Pavilion), the main character loved a female ghost, shared intellectual conversations, and held a cerebral relationship. The protagonist in *Namyeombujuji* (The Story of Visiting the Otherworld) was a scholar who repeatedly failed at exams to become an official but had such high self-esteem that he did not feel ashamed. He had intellectual discussions with the King of Hades in the otherworld and received his recognition as an outstanding scholar. The otherworld in his dream is an alternative world that admitted his value.

In *Yonggungbuyeonrok* (The Story of Visiting a Party at the Palace of the Dragon King), the sentiment is more pleasant and unlike the other works. The main character Han Saeng was invited to the underwater palace of the Dragon King, where he enjoyed pleasant entertainment including dancing and singing with good music and food. Han Saeng shows a contrasting sentiment that is unlike other protagonists who were continuously isolated in reality and obsessively depressed. However, it is within the same context in that it is a story of the main character showing the power of the alternative world, the palace of the Dragon King.

The fantasy of *Geumosinhwa* is sad and beautiful. The world of fantasy in the story occurs in the space where the protagonist confronts violence in reality. It is the place that recovers and calls attention to the meaning of life. The keyword dominating the reality is "violence." A war breaks out in the real world. The enemies of Japanese raiders and *honggeonjeok* (the enemies of Chinese wearing red turbans) appeared, murdered people, or threatened women's chastity. In the story, the war is not a task to fight against but accepted as an inevitable disaster. Yi Saeng in *Yi Saeng Gyu Jang Jeon* shed tears, sighed deeply, and recollected his past in his house, which fell into disrepair due to the war. Those days in which Yi Saeng felt happiness seemed like a dream. It is violent reality that makes happy times vanish like a dream.

A war is not the only violence in reality. Yi Saeng met his lover, Lady Choe, but could not marry her easily because of his father's opposition. The Joseon period was a patriarchal society with no concept of free love. Therefore, it was not the couple but the parents of both families who decided a marriage as their families' representatives. In other words, institution, ideology, and customs were a certain violence for young generations.

Time in the real world itself is limited, so the limits of destiny cannot be changed. This fact can be severe violence to the person directly involved. Even if someone meets a lover and spends a whole lifetime, they cannot go against destiny and the limits of time. Yi

Saeng again met Lady Choe who came back to reality as a ghost and they lived together in love. However, they had to separate again as it reached the time fixed by destiny.

In the world of *Geumosinhwa*, every moment that the main character experienced in reality was controlled by destiny and was recognized as inevitable violence. The reality is always violent, desolate, and in vain. It was the writer's sense of reality that the main characters of *Geumosinhwa* all disappeared in the real world.

The Beauty of Vanishing Things, Ontology of Extinction

There is a common factor in that all the main characters disappeared or vanished without a trace in the endings of *Geumosinhwa*. Each story's final sentence is "People say that no one knew where he went."

> *Manboksajeopogi* (Playing *Jeopo* at the Manbok Temple)
> "After Lady Choe left to the otherworld, Yang Saeng never remarried, moved to Mt. Jiri, and lived by collecting medicinal plants. Nobody knows where he ended his life."

> *Yi Saeng Gyu Jang Jeon* (The Story of Yi Saeng Peering over the Wall)
> "After her (his wife's) memorial service, Yi Saeng looked back on the past and became sick. He died in several months. People grieved over the news and everyone remembered their integrity and love."

Chwiyububyeokjeonggi (Playing Drunk in the Bubyeok Pavilion)
"As Hong Saeng woke up in surprise, (everything he experienced) was a dream. He ordered his people to bathe him and change his clothes, burn incense, and sweep the yard. Then he unfolded a mat in the yard, laid down, shortly resting his chin in his hands, and passed away. It was the 15th of September. Although his body was placed in a funeral parlor, his face did not change color even after three or four days. People said that he became a hermit because he had met one, so the color of his face never changed."

Namyeombujuji (The Story of Visiting the Otherworld)
"After waking up in surprise, he found that everything was a dream. He opened his eyes and examined everything in detail. The book was on the desk and lamplight was flickering. He thought deeply and started to arrange daily domestic chores while wondering in his mind about dying. After two or three months, Park Saeng became sick. He thought he would never survive, so he said goodbye to a doctor and a shaman, and finally passed away. In the evening when he was about to leave the world, a God appeared in a neighbor's dream and said "Your neighbor Park Saeng will be the King of Hades soon.""

Yonggungbuyeonrok (The Story of Visiting a Party at the Underwater Palace of the Dragon King)
"When Han Saeng exited the door, stars were blinking here and there, and dawn was about to break. A rooster crowed three times

and it was already about 5 o'clock. Looking at the things that he had brought in his arms, a gem that emits light in the dark and the silk *bingcho*, Han Saeng put them in a box and kept them like precious treasure. He did not show them to others often. From that time on, Han Seang never paid attention to secular honor and profit. He later went to the Mt. Myeong and no one knew where he ended his life."

Geumosinhwa is a fantasy story and a narrative of extinction. It is a story of ruin, loss, isolation, and solitude as well as a story illuminating the beauty of vanishing being. The main characters of *Geumosinhwa* commune, communicate, love, and enjoy happiness with ghosts but never reveal it. These figures are different than those who debate, battle, fight, boast, and show off in order to elevate their standing. They are the people who kept unspeakable secrets. This is because the fantasy world symbolizes the internal. At the moment that their secret expires, it will be ruined and insulted as a lie. Instead of sharing their experience, they keep it to themselves until the end of their lives. They also disappear from the reality that is hurting them and never share their whereabouts.

The main characters surrender to the fantasy world by disappearing from reality. If life itself is the will to power as Nietzsche said,[3] a protagonist's death or extinction is not a form of defeat against reality but an expression of the sincere will to power.

---

3   Nietzsche, Friedrich Wilhelm, *The Will to Power*. Translated by Kang Sunam. Cheongha, 1991, p. 48.

While adopting Walter Benjamin's definition that the true measure of life is memory,[4] it can be said that the main characters accused the problems of reality by ceasing to exist in the middle of their youth. The protagonists again speak against the violence of the world through extinction of self, which is a powerful method for proving a social meaning of individual.

Esthetics of *Yi Saeng Gyu Jang Jeon*: Communion of Spirits and Beautiful Romance

Now let's examine the narrative esthetics of *Yi Saeng Gyu Jang Jeon*. First, this work is a beautiful and sad romance novel. In Joseon period, which is the background of the novel, it was common practice that after seven years old a boy and a girl could not even sit together. Therefore, it was a violation of common knowledge for a scholar to peer over the wall of a woman's house and a woman to throw a stone with a paper of romantic poems to the scholar passing by her house. The taboo was broken. The protagonists were Yi Saeng and Lady Choe.

The main character Yi Saeng in the story had a timid, anxious, and negative personality. Unlike him, Lady Choe was bold, active, and positive. As Yi Saeng sent a passive reply to Lady Choe's poem, seducing him into a romantic relationship, she confidently said

---

4 Benjamin, Walter, *Walter Benjamin's theory of Literary Art*. Edited and translated by Ban Seong-wan. Mineumsa, 1992, p.170.

that she would take full responsibility. Two people had opposite personalities. The two enjoyed secret love. However, Yi Saeng's father felt suspicious of his son who left home at night and returned at dawn. In the end, he sent Yi Saeng to a province called Ulju, and so Yi Saeng and Lady Choe became separated. Once Lady Choe figured out the situation, she became lovesick. Choe's parents felt afraid that they would lose their precious daughter, so they arranged her marriage with Yi Saeng at last. Yi Saeng's father rejected it saying that his family was too poor to marry a daughter of a noble family. He thought that the two families were not matched for marriage. However, he allowed the marriage, because Choe family's sincerely repeated the proposal to save the daughter.

Their happiness lasted for a short time until a war with Chinese robbers broke out, *honggeonjeok*'s invasion. Yi Saeng and Lady Choe became separated on the way to evacuate. Yi Saeng felt guilty for not having saved his family, and Lady Choe was murdered while resisting a robber who tried to rape her. Yi Saeng survived alone lost in memories of the old days after he returned to his home in ruins. At that time, footsteps approached and his wife came back. She was actually a ghost. The dead spirit came back momentarily because she missed him. Yi Saeng would not meet with anybody and spent time only with his wife. If someone saw Yi Saeng, who was speaking with Lady Choe, he must have looked like a crazy man talking to himself into the air. This was because he became an autistic being who only communicated with a ghost. In other words, Yi Saeng could be considered a being who completely blocked communication with reality itself. Ironically speaking, Yi Saeng was able to communicate only with a ghost because he was a being completely excluded from reality. The only unique being that communicated with him was his wife, the appreciative being who deeply understood his internal self. However, she was not a human but a ghost.

When the main character and a ghost communicate and commune together, the ghost is not the strange other but a phantom of the main character's internal self. The appreciative friend understanding and sharing spiritual communication is the internal self that recognizes oneself in the end. The communication with a ghost is actually a soliloquy of a lonely spirit. The main characters of *Geumosinhwa*, including *Yi Saeng Gyu Jang Jeon*, all wrote poems or created writings. To them writing is a unique way of communicating with the world. The correspondents are not humans but fantastic beings such as a ghost, a King of Hades, or a Dragon King. In the characters' writings, the writer Kim Si-seup's meaning and value of writing are projected.

In the Joseon society, imaginative writings that were not based on history or scriptures were prohibited at that time. Kim Si-seup, who was a literati scholar, tried "speaking to the world" through "writing fictions," which was reflected exactly in the main character's actions. To him, writing was not the task of transferring beings into the given world and adapting them to it. It was a task of creating subjects who think for themselves and assign the values. It is an adventurous and experimental activity testing creative functions of beings. Therefore, Kim Si-seup's fictions can be understood as fantasy literature, while the fantastic factors in his fictions are interpreted as an activity creatively manifesting the internal.

Epilogue

This book starts with the story of a hero who established a nation for the first time on the Korean peninsula and finishes with the story of a weak man who disappeared, while wishing that no trace of him would be left in the world. However, it is you who decide which path you will follow. In the meantime, history and literature will frequently talk to you and ask you questions about your choices. Please enjoy these conversations, which will open the door to a meaningful path for your time here.

Translators

Lee Sun-hee

An Associate Professor of Korean Language and Culture at Wellesley College, Dr. Lee Sun-hee is a linguist who works on corpus-based analysis, Korean learner language, and genre and discourse analysis. She is the main author of *A Korean Frequency Dictionary: Core Vocabulary for Learners* (2014) and *Korean Particles and Thematic Roles* (2004). Other publications include papers and essays on various grammatical phenomena in Korean, as well as the book, *Modern Korean Syntax* (2005; original 현대국어통사론 written by Nam Ki-shim) co-translated with Allison Blodgett.

Allison Blodgett

A freelance editor, Allison Blodgett earned her Ph.D. in psycholinguistics with a specialization in human sentence processing from The Ohio State University in 2004.

Ko Yu-jin

Professor of English at Wellesley College. Dr. Ko Yu-jin is the co-editor of *Shakespeare's Sense of Character: On the Page and From the Stage* (2012) and the author of *Mutability and Division on Shakespeare's Stage* (2004). Other publications include essays on films and performances from around the globe such as "The site of burial in two Korean Hamlets," *The Shakespearean International Year book*.

Illustrator

Lee Hyun-a

A graduate of the Department of Oriental Painting, College of Fine Arts, Hongik University, Lee Hyun-a is a professional illustrator and artist. She has contributed artistic drawings to a large number of published books and has held major exhibitions of her own works.

Major Exhibitons

2015	ACAF Art Fair (Hangaram Art Museum Seoul Art Center/Seoul/2015)
2014	LA Art Fair (LA Convention Center/LA/2014)
2013~2014	Exhibition in Georgia Berlin gallery (Berlin)
2012	Miami River Art Fair (Miami Convention Center/Miami/2012)
Website	www.sosaism.com